The Market Girl's Secret

a Victorian romance saga

HOPE DAWSON

Copyright © 2021, Hope Dawson
All rights reserved.

First published worldwide
on Amazon Kindle,
in May 2021.

This paperback edition first published
in Great Britain in 2021.

ISBN: 9798510166446

This novel is a work of fiction. The characters, names, places, events and incidents in it are entirely the work of the author's imagination or used in a fictitious manner. Any resemblance or similarity to actual persons, living or dead, events or places is entirely coincidental.

No part of this work may be reproduced, stored in a retrieval system, or transmitted, in any form or by any means, without the prior permission of the author and the publisher.

www.hopedawson.com

To girls and women everywhere
– past and present –
living in toil and hardship
yet never giving up hope
and always striving for a better tomorrow.

Also by Hope Dawson:

The Forgotten Daughter
The Carter's Orphan
The Millworker's Girl
The Ratcatcher's Daughter
The Foundling With The Flowers
The Pit Brow Sisters
The Dockside Orphans
The Christmas Foundling
The Girl Below Stairs

*For more details, updates,
and to claim your free book,
please visit Hope's website:*

www.hopedawson.com

Chapter One

London, 1877

With eyes wide in amazement, little Nettie Morris looked at the bustling market that was coming to life around her. The experience never failed to overwhelm her. As always, there were sights, sounds and smells everywhere – some nice, others less so. Costermongers with loud voices were trying to draw the attention of the early morning crowd, while others exchanged pleasantries or shouted abuse at each other, depending on their mood.

Although the marketplace wasn't all that big in actual square footage, to a six-year-old girl like Nettie it felt like a complete world on its own. And as the eldest daughter of a family of costers, it was *her* world.

Despite her young age, she had already been to the market more often and spent more time there than most grownups. Mother liked to tell the story about how Nettie was barely a day old when they had taken her along for the first time, swaddled in a cloth sling so she was snuggled close to Mother's warm bosom.

And there had been plenty more occasions when she'd had to join her parents. Mostly whenever Nan was too poorly to look after the children.

Today was different however. Because today she wasn't just a visitor anymore, accompanying her parents. This would be her first proper working day at the market.

"Nettie, my love," her father declared, laying his big hand on her tiny shoulder. "On this fine day, you become a costermonger."

As if he were some heroic figure, he placed his other hand on his chest and gazed dreamily into the distance. "Just like your dear father."

She nodded her head slowly, duly impressed by his statement and the solemn tone of his voice.

"And just like your hard-working ma," Nettie's mother grunted while she and her eight-year-old son John lifted a basket of potatoes off their cart. "When you're done delivering your speech,

Henry, do you think you could lend us a hand with these heavy crates?"

"Speech? Woman, can't you see I am impressing upon our daughter the importance and the gravity of the situation? She needs to be instructed properly in the ways of the coster."

Harriet Morris rolled her eyes and continued to arrange their stall by herself. She knew it was useless to argue with her husband when he was feeling pompous like this. The man delighted in a bit of fanfare. And it was usually a bad idea to deny him any opportunity to make himself look or sound more important than he really was.

"Good morning, Mr and Mrs Morris," a priest dressed in a long black frock greeted them with a smile. "I see you have brought your eldest girl along again."

"Morning, Father Michael," Nettie's father replied warmly. "Today is a special occasion, sir. It's her first day as a coster."

"Following in her father's footsteps, is she? You must be very proud, Mr Morris."

Nettie could see her father's chest swell with pride.

"I am, Father. Nearly brought a tear to my eye, it did, this morning when I arose from bed."

Nettie's mother snorted. "Was this before or after you shouted for bacon and coffee?"

Henry threw his wife a dirty glare, but Father Michael merely laughed.

"I wish you all a successful day," he said. "And for you, my dear Nettie, good luck. Will I still see you at Sunday school now that you have a job to do?"

Before she could say anything, her father answered the question for her. "I'm afraid Sunday mornings are a busy time for us, Father. People get their wages the day before, which means they've got money to spend on groceries again."

"Of course," the priest nodded kindly.

Nettie hadn't thought of that particular consequence yet. But now it made her sad. She loved Sunday school. They sang songs, learned their letters and numbers, and there would always be something nice to eat and drink. But more importantly, Father Michael and the nuns were kind to the children. And kindness was rare in the hard world Nettie lived in.

Her sadness must have shown on her face, she thought, because the priest gave her a sorry, sympathetic look.

"Besides," her father continued, "she already knows how to read and write, and she can do her numbers. That's good enough for a market girl. No need to turn her into a learned doctor."

He laughed at his own witty remark, and the priest smiled along politely.

"Well, I shan't keep you any longer," Father Michael said cheerfully. "I am sure you brave people have a long day ahead of you."

He tipped his broad-brimmed hat to them and continued on his way, greeting familiar faces as he went.

"Does Father Michael work at the market as well?" Nettie asked.

"No, he doesn't, child."

"Then why is he here?"

"I suppose he visits the market to tend to his flock."

"Which flock is that, Father? I don't see any sheep around."

"Not sheep, you silly girl. We are his flock."

"But we're people. How can we be his flock if we're not sheep?"

"It's just something people say," her father bristled. "Priests are like shepherds tending their flock of faithful."

"Who are the faithful?"

"Those are the people who believe in God."

"Do we believe in God, Father?"

Henry Morris became increasingly annoyed at his daughter's incessant questions. He wasn't much of a listener and preferred to do most of the talking himself.

"We believe in many things, Nettie. Especially things that make us money."

After he had chuckled at his clever note, he then felt the need to be more serious about a subject as lofty as religion.

"But Father Michael and his nuns do good work," he said. "They look after the poorest among us, as well as the sick and the dying. That's why we like them. They are fine and decent people."

"Very kind too."

"That's right. Being kind is important."

"Is that why you are always so kind to our customers, Father?"

"Indeed, it is." Henry Morris nodded gravely, before chuckling again. "That, and because a friendly smile helps to loosen the purse." He made the money gesture between his fingers and laughed.

Nettie nodded. Her father was so wise, she thought, her heart full of awe and respect for him. She resolved that she would listen to his every word, watch his every move, and learn all the tricks of the trade. So she would one day become as good a coster as her father.

"You know, Nettie," he said, resting a fatherly hand on her shoulder again. "Some people look down upon us. Hawkers, they call us."

She didn't understand that word. But the way her father said it, she guessed it wasn't nice. And definitely not something she wanted to be called.

The idea that anyone might think she wasn't a good person simply because of what her family did for a living was new to her.

New and uncomfortable.

"But we are market people, Father. Isn't that a good thing to be then?"

"Yes, we are. And yes, it is! The way I see it, we are essential for the very survival of this city."

With a grand gesture, he waved at their surroundings. "We feed the population, through the vegetables and fruits we sell. Without us, the good people of London would starve."

Nettie hadn't thought of it like that before. And it did make their profession sound quite important.

"People may mock us," her father proclaimed. "But us costers, we contribute to the prosperity of the city on a daily basis. Which makes us noble folk and a fine breed indeed."

"Yeah, you tell 'em, Henry," a nearby bread seller laughed.

Taking his reaction for agreement, Nettie's father nodded at the man in acknowledgement. Then he bent down and whispered in her ear.

"And we're certainly finer and more noble than some. Take those dirty blighters for instance."

With a dark look in his eye, he pointed at a man and a young boy standing twenty or so yards away from them. They had an old cart heaped high with all manner of rags, clothes, shoes, and a wide variety of odd bits and bobs.

"Who are they, Father?"

"Ragmen, my darling." Henry Morris spat on the ground in disgust. "And those two are the filthiest and most dishonest of them all. Kirby, their family is called. Remember their name. And avoid them and their ilk at all cost."

Holding her breath, Nettie nodded. She didn't know why Mr Kirby and his son were bad, but if her father said so, then that's what she would believe.

"What do ragmen do, Father?"

"They buy and sell rags," he said as if it was the most offensive thing imaginable. "Old clothes or anything else people want to get rid of, the ragmen will buy it for cheap and then sell it for a profit."

That didn't sound too bad to Nettie. And not unlike what her father did. The only difference was he bought fruit and vegetables from the wholesalers and then sold his produce on the market for more money than he had paid for it.

"And they search through dustbins too," her father continued, pinching his nose. "Anything they think they can turn into a profit, they'll take with them, clean it and then sell it."

"Do they make a lot of money from that? Are they rich?"

Henry Morris scoffed. "They've probably got more money than they're willing to show. But their filthy trade is a dishonest one. So any money they have is tainted."

Together, they stared at Mr Kirby and his son – her father with an evil glare, Nettie more with intrigue and fascination. She was learning so much about the world today!

She wondered if Mr Kirby's son was having his first day on the job as well. He looked slightly older than her, but not by much. Maybe a year or two, like her brother John. His face was dirty and his clothes were too big, she noticed.

Suddenly, the boy caught her staring at him. He pulled an ugly face and stuck his tongue out at her.

Surprised, Nettie blushed and looked away. It wasn't nice of him to stick his tongue out like that, she thought. But then again, she had been staring at him and that wasn't nice either. So she made up her mind that this now made them even.

The rest of the day, she worked hard. Handing customers their orders, smiling at people walking by, calling out to the crowd about the big potatoes and juicy apples they simply had to try. Nettie wanted to do it all. So she would become the best market girl in the world.

But no matter how busy she got, the image of the boy sticking his tongue out never quite left her mind. Her father clearly didn't like the Kirby family. So did that mean they didn't like her family either? Was that why Mr Kirby's son had pulled a face at her?

If they had been costermongers as well, would they have been friends?

And what sort of person would she have been if her family had been ragmen instead?

Questions like that often bothered her. And she knew her father didn't like answering them. So she never asked.

Chapter Two

Six years later...

With the ease and nimbleness that came from years of experience, Nettie moved through the rowdy crowd at the public house. Men, women and children alike were engaged in their usual evening routine that consisted of drinking, shouting, singing and other activities that involved a lot of raucous noisemaking.

Mainly though, they were drinking.

And Nettie knew that was good for business. She didn't care much for beer herself, although it was usually safer to drink than the water they fetched at the pump in their street. But once the patrons at the pub had drunk two or three pints of ale, they would be more likely to spend a few coins on the small bags of nuts she and her younger sisters were selling.

She kept one eye on Hannah and Jane, who were going round the tables nearer the door, while she worked the far corners. Tables with loud and inebriated men would sometimes fetch the best profits, but men like that also came with a risk. At twelve years old, Nettie knew how to handle them however.

"Care for some nuts, good sirs?" she asked with a smile at a table with three men who seemed cheerful enough.

"Are they any good?" one of them asked.

"They're the best, sir. My mother roasted them herself, slowly over a gentle fire. Brings out the flavour more."

"You sound like you know your nuts," one of the others laughed.

"I take my business very seriously, sir," she replied with the confidence of a seasoned coster. "Would you like to taste one?"

She offered each of them a nut, and smiled as they accepted the free treat. Her father hated it when she gave things away for free. But experience had taught her it helped to sell more.

"You're right," the first man said. "They are delicious. I think I'll have a small bag."

"As will I," the second customer chimed in.

Which meant the third man now felt obliged to follow suit, lest his drinking companions thought he was a miser.

"Say, aren't you a Morris girl?" he asked when he had paid her.

"I am indeed, sir. Henry Morris is my father."

He winked. "I can see where you get your sales talent from then."

"Much better looking than her old pa though," the second one laughed, before he hungrily threw back a handful of nuts into his mouth.

She smiled and nodded at the compliments. "Thank you, good sirs. Enjoy your evening, and I hope you will buy from me again."

"With a pretty little angel face like yours? Of course we will, love."

Just as she turned to leave, the third man touched her elbow and said, "I believe your father is here as well, incidentally." He pointed at a table further down. "You might want to go and have a look, before old Henry gets himself into trouble again."

Nettie saw her father sitting at a table with several other men. As usual, Henry Morris was doing most of the talking. She couldn't hear what exactly he was saying, and she was sure it was meaningless nonsense anyway. But the sound of his voice carried far, even in the busy alehouse.

As she approached his small group, she noticed the collection of jugs and tankards sitting in front of them. No doubt he had been overly generous again in buying beer for his friends. Wanting to be liked and respected by his peers was her father's weakness. And a costly one too.

"Hello, Father," she greeted him flatly.

Looking up in the middle of the story he was telling with his trademark grand gestures, he seemed surprised yet delighted to see her.

"Oh, hullooo, my darling angel!"

The twinkling look in his eyes and the smell of his breath told her he had been drinking a lot of ale. She dreaded to think how much of their hard-earned money he had already spent.

"Will you be coming home soon?" she asked. Which was her polite way of suggesting that maybe he'd had enough to drink and he should stop.

"Sweet Lord, doesn't she sound just like her mother?" Henry Morris proclaimed, earning the other men's laughter.

"Father, I'm serious. It's late, and tomorrow you'll need to rise early to be in time for the market."

"I know, dear. I know. I was only teasing you. But me and my friend the pie maker here, we were just about to conclude a... business agreement."

Nettie eyed her father and his so-called friend suspiciously. "What kind of business agreement?"

"The kind we settle with cards," the pie maker grinned, tapping a fat finger on the playing cards that were lying face down on the table.

A card game, she sighed to herself. He was playing cards for money – again. Between his drinking and his gambling, her father regularly lost over half of their earnings.

"So, Henry," the pie maker said. "What will it be? Is your hand strong enough, do you think?"

"But of course it is, my dear man," Nettie's father boasted.

"So you agree to our stakes then? If you win, you get half of tomorrow's stock of pies. If I win, I get all of your takings from today."

Nettie gasped. Her father was betting a full day's worth of earnings on a card game?!

"Father, no!" she begged, grabbing his shoulder fearfully.

"Don't interfere in men's business, Nettie," he bristled, shaking off her hand. "Yes, I agree to those stakes, dear fellow. In fact," –he took a swig of his ale– "I shall double them! Your entire stock of pies against *two* days of my earnings."

The pie maker's grin grew even wider. "Let's see those cards of yours then."

Equally confident, the two men turned their cards over, revealing their hands. Laughter broke out, the pie maker called for more beer, and her father's face dropped.

He had lost.

Laughing, the other men clapped her father on the shoulder. To them, this was just a joke. Part of the entertainment of the evening.

But for Nettie and her family, games like these spelled disaster. Because they needed every penny to pay the rent, keep food on the table and buy produce from the wholesalers each day.

"Father, you've just lost this week's rent money," she hissed at him.

"A minor setback," he said. He was smiling and trying to sound unaffected by his substantial loss. But she could see the pearls of sweat that had broken out on his brow.

"Two days of earnings isn't minor, Father!"

"Bah, you think that because you're a woman, Nettie. Us men, we look at the bigger perspective of things. Two days is nothing. It's a risk of the trade any successful businessman should be willing to take."

Unable to control her temper in the face of so much uncaring ignorance, she angrily stamped her feet.

The pie maker laughed, and said, "I like the risks you take, Henry. Now kindly give me my winnings."

Nettie's father reluctantly emptied the contents of his leather pouch into the palms of the man's outstretched hands.

Nettie was fuming on the inside. Why did she and her sisters have to work day and night, only for him to throw half of it away at the pub? When her father got up, she glared at him with the sort of hostile force only a twelve-year-old daughter could harness.

"Don't look at me like that, Nettie. Remember, I am your father."

Gleefully, she detected a hint of fear in his voice.

"Besides," he continued as he pressed past her, "it would have been a great deal if I had pulled it off."

"But you didn't pull it off, did you?" she shouted, pursuing him through the crowd.

"Who cares for such details?"

"We needed that money, Father."

He stopped and turned around, pretending not to have heard her accusing tone.

"Speaking of money, how much have you got on you? I still need to pay for the beer."

Nettie rolled her eyes. She couldn't believe he had the audacity to ask her for money after he had wasted his in a card game. But he was impatiently holding out his hand, so she gave him her small pouch of coins.

"Not an awful lot, is there?" he grumbled after he had quickly inspected its contents. "Fetch your sisters and get their money as well, will you?"

She wanted to protest. "Father, you can't—"

"If that doesn't cover my beer tab, I'm sure old Bill won't mind me paying the rest tomorrow evening. He knows I'm good for it."

"And how exactly will we be paying the rent this week?"

Henry Morris shrugged. "Cut back on our expenses obviously. There are bound to be certain luxuries and niceties we can do without for a week or two."

"Like food you mean?"

Angrily, her father placed his clenched fists on his hips. "Nettie, I've had enough of this rude insolence of yours! As the head of this family, I shall be treated with the respect I rightly deserve. What would your poor mother say if she heard you talking to me like that?"

"I'm more interested in what she will say when she hears you lost our rent money in a card game," she grinned defiantly.

"Nothing at all, that's what," her father said, sticking out a haughty chin. "As my loyal and devoted wife, your mother knows her place. So she won't say anything about this unfortunate setback and she will continue to trust in my superior judgement."

He was right about the first part, Nettie thought. Harriet Morris would probably sigh and roll her eyes, and that would be it. But trust his judgement? Nettie found that hard to believe. She suspected her mother tolerated rather than respected or trusted her husband.

Nettie vowed that when she grew up, she wouldn't give up and surrender as easily. Not to her father, or any other man.

Chapter Three

Not a word was uttered while Mother placed the pot that contained their dinner on the table. But the glowering expression on the faces of Nettie and the other three Morris children said it all. As did the cold glare their mother shot in her husband's direction.

Henry Morris however pretended there wasn't a cloud in the sky. He lifted the lid off the pot and breathed in the aroma as if it was a divine and delicious scent.

"Ah, potatoes and turnips," he sighed happily.

"Of course," Nettie's older brother John muttered. "What else would it be? We haven't eaten anything but potatoes and turnips for over a week."

"But today is special, lad. Today, your mother has made some gravy to accompany our potatoes. It's a veritable feast, I tell you."

He laughed at his own joke, but he stopped when he saw no one was joining in.

"Oh, will you all cheer up! I am merely trying to make light of an unfortunate situation. A fleeting, temporary moment of scarcity. That's all this is."

"And who's to blame for that scarcity but you, Father?" John asked bitterly.

You took the words right out of my mouth, brother dear, Nettie thought. Whenever he was around, she could rely on John to tell their father the hard truth. Saving her the trouble.

Helping himself to two of the largest potatoes, their father bristled, "I've had enough of your big mouth, John."

"And I've had enough of your boasting and wastefulness, Father."

Everyone fell silent around the table.

"John, dear," Mother said softly. Nettie knew their mother was on their side in this matter. But in her role as both mother and wife, Harriet Morris often felt it was her duty to keep the peace between her children and her husband. So now she was trying to defuse this tense situation, before it got out of hand.

But John wasn't having any of it.

"No, I mean it, Mother. It's not fair that you, me and the girls should work so hard to earn a pittance, while he throws it all away on drinking and gambling. As soon as he's got a few coins rattling in his pocket, he needs to waste it on ale and card games."

"I lose one small wager and now you make it seem as if I'm a drunkard and a gambler," Father scoffed.

"Firstly, it wasn't a small wager, because you lost two whole days worth of our earnings. And secondly, it wasn't exactly the first time either."

"Be that as it may, I shall not sit here and let you insult me. As your father and the head of this family, my word is to be obeyed and respected."

John let out a disdainful huffing sound.

"What's that, son?" Father asked, cocking an ear. "I do believe I heard you making a noise."

"Henry, please," Mother pleaded. "The boy is merely a bit grumpy because he's hungry."

"Ha! Then let him work harder for his food, the arrogant ingrate."

John banged his fist on the table, startling the girls. Jane anxiously shifted closer to Nettie, who put her arm around her youngest sister.

"That's exactly what I will do, Father!"

Henry Morris eyed his son suspiciously. Something about the defiant tone in John's voice troubled him. "Good. Glad you're seeing sense."

"Yes," John continued with a grin, "I'll work hard for *my* food. But I won't be working to support your bad habits any longer."

"What's that supposed to mean?"

"It means, dear Father, that I've made a decision. I'm striking out on my own. I'll sell fruit and veg myself from now on. And I'm keeping all my profits. Starting tomorrow, I'll be my own boss."

Nettie held her breath, while their father's eyes grew wide and his face turned red with anger.

"You traitor! How dare you?"

"I'm tired of going to bed with an empty belly, just because you insist on filling yours with beer every day."

"Drinking beer is every man's right! And besides, it's needed to maintain good relations with my fellow costers and the wider community."

"Whatever you say, Father. But as from tomorrow, I'm not paying for it anymore. I want to start making my own money, seeing as you can't seem to hold on to it."

"You'll have to buy your own produce from the wholesalers."

"I know where to find them. We go there every morning, remember?"

"They won't want to do business with you. Not if I tell them how you have betrayed me."

"Do you honestly believe they'll care? They will take my money just as gladly as anyone else's."

"I forbid it."

"You can't stop me."

"I shan't tolerate my own son becoming a competitor while he sleeps under my roof and eats at my table."

"Now, Henry dear," his wife quickly intervened. "Don't be so hasty. Perhaps we should all take a moment to think this over."

"Don't need to," he said smugly. "My decision is final. I don't want him living in this house if he insists on pursuing this foolish idea of his."

"Henry, you can't–"

But John interrupted his mother. "It's fine, Mother. If that's his final word, then I have one for him too." He stood up and looked his father straight in the eye.

"Goodbye," he said, sounding very confident.

"John, no!" Harriet Morris wanted to stop her son from walking away. But her husband had made up his mind.

"Out," he said.

"No!" Mother hid her face with her apron, muffling her sobbing cries. Nettie could see Jane's lip was trembling, and she had to fight back her own tears.

"Gladly," John growled. "I'll get my things and leave."

"No, you won't," Father said. "I paid for all your clothes and everything you own. You're not taking anything that my money bought."

"Henry Morris," their mother spoke sternly. "Have some decency! The boy has worked for that money just as hard as the rest of us. John, take what you need, dear. And I'll give you a blanket to wrap it in."

"A blanket?" their father protested. "Let him buy his own, I say."

"And I say I'm giving him a blanket. If you insist on throwing our boy out on the street, the least we can do is give him something to keep warm."

"In that case," he said as he too got up, "I shall be taking myself to The Boar's Head for an ale or two." With his nose up in the air, he looked round the table. "If anyone else is thinking of defying my will, they'd best be gone from this house by the time I get back."

Strutting like a peacock, he went to the door, grabbed his coat and hat and stepped outside.

Jane started crying.

"I'll gather my things," John said.

"And don't forget to take a blanket, lad," Mother replied. "Make sure you get a big one that's nice and warm, you hear?"

John kissed his mother on the cheek and went to the old family wardrobe with the creaky doors. He didn't have much, so it didn't take him long to put all his belongings in the blanket he had chosen.

"Well, that's it then. I'm off," he stated as if he was only popping out for a pint of milk.

"Good luck to you, lad," Mother replied, putting on a brave face.

"John," Nettie said, with a fearful Jane still clinging on to her. She didn't want her older brother to leave.

"Goodbye, Nettie. To you too, Hannah. And Jane, you be a good girl, all right?"

Little Jane nodded, tears running down her face. The nine-year-old girl knew she was losing her big brother. They were all losing him.

"John, wait," Nettie said. Gently, she untangled herself from Jane's grip and passed her youngest sister to her sibling Hannah.

"Don't try to change my mind, Nettie. Save your breath." He put on his cap and opened the door.

"Then at least let me walk with you for a little while." Quickly, she got up and followed him outside.

"John, I'm worried," she said as her brother confidently strolled along the street with his few belongings slung over his shoulder. "You're only fourteen."

"I'm fourteen *already*, you mean. That's old enough to work."

"But what will you do? Where will you sleep?"

"With friends. I know a couple of lads who've done the same. They told me I could share their room with them. Makes the rent more affordable. The more the merrier, they said."

He laughed and Nettie could have sworn she detected a spring in his step.

"You're really serious about this, aren't you?"

"Sure am. You're welcome to join me. Don't tell me you haven't thought of getting away from the old fool."

She took his sleeve and the two of them stopped, while she stared at the ground. "I have. But for me it's different."

"How so?"

"You're a boy. Nearly a man, I suppose. For you, these things are easy. But I'm a girl, John. My best chance to escape is to find a good husband some day."

"So start looking."

"I'm too young, you know that. And it's not like there's a great supply of good men around these parts. Everybody is just as miserable and poor."

John shrugged. "Suit yourself, Nettie." Seeing her sad face, he softened up a bit. "Take good care of your sisters, will you? And look after Mother for me. Please?"

She nodded, unable to say much for fear of bursting out in tears, which she knew he would hate.

"You'd better head back home now. Goodbye, Nettie."

"Goodbye, John."

He smiled at her one last time and then he continued on his way. Nettie stood and watched him for a while, until he rounded a corner in the distance.

Her only brother had disappeared from her life. And it was because of their father's ludicrous behaviour. She loved John. But now he was gone. She shuddered and wondered if she would ever see him again.

This should never have happened, her angry mind raged. *It's all Father's fault!*

She caught herself clenching her fists so tight her knuckles turned white.

No, she told herself. She wouldn't give in to that feeling. Hatred was wrong. It was easy to hate someone when they had hurt you or wronged you. But as Father Michael often reminded them, hatred only ever led to more pain and suffering.

Still she wondered though. Why was she the one who had to feel all the pain and do all the suffering?

Chapter Four

"You dirty little rat!"

George Kirby's voice thundered through their rented room on the ground floor, and William was certain everyone in the building could hear his father's angry shouting. But he also knew hardly anyone would take notice, since this sort of thing was almost a daily occurrence.

That didn't make the experience any less unpleasant however. Especially when William himself was the object of his father's rage. He just hoped the violence would remain limited to words this time.

"Stealing from me, your own father?! How dare you?"

"I didn't steal anything from you," William shot back. Past experience had taught him it was useless for him to try and defend himself from outbursts like these. But he couldn't stand the injustice of it either, so he felt compelled to speak the truth.

George Kirby wasn't interested in the truth unfortunately. And he made that point by hitting out at his son. The palm of his hand connected with the boy's face.

"Liar! Then what are these?"

He held up a burlap sack and shook it angrily in front of his son's face.

"I didn't steal any of it," William said. "That's all mine."

"Yours?"

"Everything in that bag is stuff I found myself."

"Finding things is what a ragman does for a living. Why are these in a bag that you kept tucked away behind your bed, you sneaky runt?"

William knew his reply would enrage his father further. But he decided he was beyond caring at this point, so he simply blurted it out.

"Because I wanted to sell them myself."

"You what?!"

William hadn't thought his father could have turned even more purplish red with anger. But he did.

"And I suppose you weren't going to hand over the money to me, were you?"

Might as well make my stand now, William told himself.

Gathering up his courage, he stopped looking at his feet, raised his head instead and stared his father in the eye. "No, I was planning on keeping the money."

There was noticeably more force behind the hand that hit his face this time. William thought he heard his little brother Joseph whimper in the corner of the room, where his two younger brothers sat cowering with their mother. For their sake, more than for his own pride or feelings, he was determined not to show any pain or fear.

"You thief," his father spat. "How is that not stealing? Tell me that!"

"It's not stealing because I didn't take anything from you! I merely kept those things to myself, so I'd have a bit of money in my pocket."

Again, his father's hand lashed out. George Kirby was a stocky and brutal man. But William was too angry by now to notice much of the pain his father was inflicting.

"What do you need money in your pocket for? Don't I provide for you? Don't I feed, clothe and care for this family?"

Only because we can't work for you if we're naked and starving, William silently grumbled to himself. His father was notoriously stingy as well as cruel. In the Kirby household, clothes that hadn't been mended at least five times over were something to be sold for profit, not worn.

"I'll teach you to steal from me, you miserable worm," his father said menacingly. He undid his belt and slid it out of its loops. "Turn around."

"George, no," his wife pleaded. "Surely, that's not necessary."

"Shut your mouth, Mary. Or I'll give you a thrashing as well. The lad clearly needs a lesson. And there's only one way boys learn. The hard way."

He wrapped his belt around his fist a few times and looked at his son. "Turn around and bend over."

William stared coldly at his father... and then obeyed. His punishment was inevitable, and anything he said would only make his father hit him harder and longer. So he figured they might as well get it over with.

"Thomas and Joseph," their father said to his other two sons. "I want you both to watch this. No turning away, do you hear me? This is what happens to anyone who takes what's mine."

One by one, the belt lashes started coming down on William's back and buttocks. Each time the belt struck him, a hot and burning pain flashed through William's entire body. After the third lash, tears came to his eyes. He didn't want to cry – so he could at least deny his father the pleasure of seeing him suffer – but the pain was too intense. It felt like the back of his body was on fire. And still the lashes kept coming.

The only real effect however was that William despised his father even more. Every hit that bit into his tender flesh only served to fuel the hatred inside him. Gnashing his teeth, he focused on that feeling of loathing to help him drown out the pain.

And then the lashes stopped. Behind him, William could hear his father catching his breath. Slowly, he tried to straighten his back again, as good as he possibly could despite the agony he was in.

"I can't tell you how disappointed I am in you, son," his father growled. "To think it should come to this. If I ever catch you stealing from me again, I'll kick you out of my house. If I don't kill you first."

I might not give you the chance, William thought. *I might just decide to leave all by myself before that happens.*

"Well?! What have you got to say for yourself?"

"You won't catch me stealing again, Father."

Because I'll be more careful in the future.

He had been foolish to keep those items to himself for so long. He should have sold them sooner. Money was easier to hide. But he wouldn't be making that mistake again. The memory of this lashing would help to remind him.

"Good," his father grumbled while he put his belt around his waist again.

In the corner, Joseph was sobbing quietly. Their mother tried to muffle the sound by pressing her youngest son's head to her chest.

But George Kirby had heard, causing his irritation to flare up once more.

"Will you stop crying, Joseph? Unless you want to feel my belt as well? Maybe that would harden you up a bit."

"The boy is merely frightened, George," his wife said, nervously stroking her son's hair in an attempt to sooth him.

"Frightened, bah. Have you given me nothing but pitiful weaklings then, Mary?"

He slapped his youngest son on the head, but their mother tried to turn away and shield Joseph from harm.

"Why can't you all be more like your cousin Robert?" their father raged at his three boys. "I'd give my left arm to have a son like him."

William was more than familiar with his father's love for Robert. To George Kirby's eyes, his favourite nephew embodied everything his own sons were not. And he took every opportunity to compare them to him.

But William didn't like Robert. They were both fourteen and their features betrayed they were close relatives. Their personalities couldn't have been more different though. Robert was a mean and vicious troublemaker who loved to get into fights. Which was probably part of the reason why his father loved him so much.

"I'm off to the pub," George Kirby announced. "Where I can enjoy the company of people who understand what it means to be a man."

When he slammed the door behind him, they all breathed out in relief. There was no telling how drunk and in what sort of mood their father would be when he got back. But for the next few hours at least, their home would be peaceful.

"I'm sorry, Mother," William apologised.

"That was a foolish thing to do, dear," she said. "Hiding those things from your father like that." There was no bitterness or blame in her voice. Merely concern, and a hint of resignation. "You know how short-tempered he is."

"But I want to be prepared for the future, Mother. I won't always be living under Father's roof. One day, I'll be old enough to start my own family. And chances are he will have thrown me out before that happens. Either way,

I want to have a bit of money when that time comes."

She nodded. "I understand, dear. And you won't hear me saying you're wrong to try. But please be more cautious next time."

"I will."

Wincing from his aching back, he went over to her and kissed his mother on the forehead.

His youngest brother Joseph looked up at him and asked, "Does that mean you'll be leaving us, William?"

"Eventually, yes. But not today, little brother."

"I'd be very sad if you left."

"Yeah, William," his brother Thomas said. "If you leave, what's to become of us?"

"Lads, I'm your big brother, so I will always try to look after you. But you also need to learn to stand on your own two feet, you hear?"

Thomas nodded and Joseph took hold of his eldest brother's sleeve. "I promise I'll become just as brave and as honest as you are, William," he said.

"Same," Thomas agreed.

Smiling, William drew his brothers close to him and gave them both a squeeze with his arms around them.

He would miss them, he knew.

But no matter how much he loved them and his mother, he wouldn't let those feelings get in the way when his chance to escape came round.

Chapter Five

Years later...

Nettie smiled when she rounded the corner and their house came into sight. She was tired and her feet ached from walking several miles. But the small money pouch in her pocket felt pleasingly full, which made up for the physical discomfort she had to endure. Running deliveries for customers had been her idea. At the start, Father had been opposed to it, mainly since the idea wasn't his – which naturally, in his mind, meant it couldn't be any good. They were costermongers, he had said, and the market was their natural environment. People should come to them, he claimed, not the other way around.

But Nettie's plan had proven a success nonetheless. Several times a week, while her parents and her two sisters worked at the market, she delivered orders at a number of regular addresses. Most of them were bigger houses where the staff didn't have much time to venture out to the market themselves. So the housekeepers at these addresses didn't mind paying a few pennies more for the convenience of getting their fruit and vegetables delivered to the door.

And despite its success, Father still couldn't bring himself to acknowledge it. Probably because they were using the money to pay for household expenses more essential than ale and card games in the pub, she grinned to herself.

A sudden wolf whistle from across the street made her look up. A group of older boys and young men were sitting on a short flight of steps, just loafing about.

"Hey, Nettie," one of them called out. "Looking pretty as ever with that smile of yours."

They were fairly harmless and she had known most of them since they were children. But she also knew better than to engage with them.

"Why don't you come and join us?" another one said. "We could do with some good-looking company."

"No, thank you," she replied politely as she continued to walk home.

"Oww, you're breaking my heart, love," the first lad said, clasping both his hands over his chest.

Looking over her shoulder, she joked, "I didn't know you even had a heart, Charlie. And besides, that's the wrong side of your chest."

The group roared with laughter. Returning their banter was the best way to deal with them, she had learned. It showed them that verbally, she was just as quick and just as strong as them.

Slipping into the hallway of their tenement, she wished her own father was as easy to handle. The sound of his booming voice greeted her before she had entered their room. He sounded cheerful and she wondered if perhaps that meant he was drunk again or merely pontificating at whoever else was in the room with him.

"Nettie dearest," he beamed when she came in. "I was just telling your mother about a truly brilliant idea I've had."

Unseen behind his back, Mother rolled her eyes at her eldest daughter. But it was always better to humour him when he was in this sort of mood. So Nettie cocked her head and waited for him to explain.

"It's something that will make us money," he said. "Good money too. Not this penny scraping business of lugging fresh produce across town."

"Oooh," she cooed. "I can tell it's going to be good simply by the excited tone of your voice."

The great thing about her father was that he hardly ever noticed when you were mocking him. Self-important people were like that. Too full of themselves to suspect you might be laughing at them.

"We are going to add a new line of goods to our business," he declared as proudly as if he were announcing some royal decree.

"A new variety of potatoes?" she teased.

"Nothing like that at all, dear. No, next to our vegetables and fruit, we will also start selling pots and pans and crockery."

He paused, waiting for her praise. When none was forthcoming straight away, he smiled and said, "I can see you're impressed by the brilliance of my plan."

"Pots and pans?" she asked.

"Everything one needs to prepare a fine meal. That's what the Morris family will be offering."

"I see. And where will we acquire these goods?"

"We'll buy them – brand new obviously. None of this dirty ragmen stuff others have discarded and thrown away."

"Brand new?! But that's going to be expensive. We simply haven't got that kind of money, Father. We can't even afford new clothes."

"And that's precisely why we need a plan like mine. So we can earn more money. The profit margin on these pots and pans will be much higher."

"But we need to buy them first!" She was growing exasperated with how poorly he seemed to understand such basic matters. "Where are we going to get that money from?"

"We'll borrow it."

"More debts? Father, do you think that's wise?"

"You women folk," he tutted. "It's clear you don't grasp how business and finance works. Borrowing money so you can use it to make more money – that's what all successful and wealthy people do."

"You're neither successful nor wealthy!"

"But we will be once we put this plan of mine into action."

"Father, please. Don't. It's too much risk."

"Nonsense, Nettie. Have some faith. My plan can't fail."

"What if people don't want to buy pots and pans from us?"

"Why wouldn't they? Our goods will be of the finest quality."

"Our customers are used to us selling vegetables and fruit. They might not need pots and pans. And they probably don't have the money for it either."

"But those fancy houses you deliver to might."

"Father–"

"No, Nettie. My mind's made up. We are going to do this and it will work. You'll see. In no time at all, we shall have the means to expand even further. We'll be able to hire young lads to do all the hard work for us, while we sit back and enjoy life."

"I knew that's what this was about. You growing fat and drinking beer in the pub all day long."

"I take offence at your insinuations, Nettie," he huffed. "Would you deny your poor father material comfort and some well-deserved rest in his old age?"

"I'm thinking more of our current situation. Things are hard enough as they stand. And yet here you are, wanting to pile even more debt on our shoulders."

"Bah, you're just jealous because my idea is better than your delivery foolishness. How dreadfully petty of you. Short-sighted too."

He grabbed his coat and went to the door.

"But that's a woman for you, I guess. I'm going to see a few moneylenders and then I shall celebrate my new business venture in the company of men who appreciate my genius."

"The alehouse, you mean?"

He slammed the door angrily, and Nettie sighed.

"Mother, we ought to stop him."

"You know what your father is like, dear. Once he gets something in that big empty head of his, there's no stopping him."

"But it's bound to go horribly wrong! This will end badly, like most of his plans."

"Yes, you're probably right, dear."

"Doesn't that worry you?" She couldn't understand how her mother managed to stay so indifferent and impassive in the face of Father's never-ending stream of stupid ideas.

"You learn to stop worrying about matters you can't control, Nettie. And a husband is most definitely one of the things beyond a woman's control."

"In that case, I'm not sure I'll ever want one."

Harriet Morris smiled.

"When the right man comes along and whispers sweet promises in your ear, I'm sure you'll change your opinion. I know I did."

And what a mess it has landed you in, Nettie thought sadly. She hoped she would be smarter when her time came. The last thing she needed was for some smooth-talking Romeo to waltz into her life and turn her world upside down.

Chapter Six

Grinning mischievously, Nettie splashed some water from the wooden tub onto the bare back of her youngest sister. Jane shrieked and then the three of them giggled.

"That water's cold, Nettie!"

"Don't be silly. It's not cold." Nettie put her hand in their bath to feel the temperature of the water. "Maybe a bit lukewarm. Here, check for yourself."

Quickly taking her hand out of the water, Nettie shook it in Jane's direction, sending cool droplets flying towards her. Again, her sister shrieked, and again they all laughed.

"The water was still fine when I just had my bath," Hannah teased.

"And I'm sure it was nice and hot when Nettie had hers first," Jane said. "Why do I always have to go last?"

"Because you're the youngest, my dear baby sister," Hannah chuckled.

Jane stuck her tongue out. "I'm not your baby sister anymore. I'm sixteen."

"Still the youngest though," Hannah giggled.

"Come on, Jane," Nettie said. "Your turn. Hop in so I can wash your hair. And be grateful you only have to share the bath water with Hannah and me. Imagine Father would've been around to have his bath as well this evening."

"Eeew!" Her sisters let out cries of disgust.

The sound of their laughter filled the small kitchen.

"Girls," Mother called from outside. "If you're making a mess in there, you're not leaving until you've cleaned everything up and my kitchen is spotless and clean again, do you hear?"

"Yes, Mother," Nettie replied with a smile.

She started washing her sister's hair once the girl was sitting in the tub.

Hannah was busy combing her long, wet hair. "Why is Mother in such a bad mood?" she whispered. "She's been like that all week long."

"Hmm, you can't really blame her," Nettie said while working up a foam on her youngest sister's head. "Not this week."

"What's so special about this week then?"

"You mean, you've forgotten?"

"Forgotten what?"

Nettie glanced outside to see if their mother wouldn't be coming in and then lowered her voice. "It's the anniversary of John's death. Don't you remember?"

"Oh, yes." Hannah lowered her eyes. "I forgot it was around this time he... You know. That we heard."

A sad mood descended over the kitchen.

"Sometimes, I have trouble remembering what John looked like," Jane said guiltily.

"Don't feel bad, sweetie," Nettie replied while she started rinsing her sister's hair. "You were so much younger when he left. We all were."

They had all been children, the three of them, when their father had banished John from their home. But Nettie remembered every single detail of it. She could still see him walking away, out of their street and out of their lives.

After that, she had only occasionally caught glimpses of her brother at the market. Or she would hear bits of news about him from other people. They usually told a sad story of John struggling to make a living.

Then, just over eighteen months after he had left, word reached them that John was dead. To make the pain of his loss even worse, it turned out it had been a pointless death over something trivial. Homeless, he had got into an argument with a drunk vagrant over some stale bread. Things turned violent, the drunk pulled a knife and that was the end of John Morris.

Their mother had been devastated.

Father however, had merely scoffed. "That's what happens to people who turn their back on their family," he had said.

At the time, no one had dared to remind him that *he* had been the cause for John's departure.

But Nettie remembered. All of it.

She took a deep breath, held it for a heartbeat or two and then let it out again in a long sigh. The mood had suddenly turned silent, and Nettie suspected her sisters were having similar thoughts.

It wasn't just the sadness of having lost their brother. The circumstances in which he had been forced to leave were equally painful. If not more so.

And they all knew who was to blame for that.

Speak of the devil, she thought when they heard their father's voice in the small courtyard, loud and boisterous as always.

"Hellooo, dearest wife of mine," he boomed. "Your husband has returned."

"Father's home," Jane said.

"And it sounds like he's been drinking," Hannah replied. "Again."

"Father," Nettie called out. "Don't come inside. We're having our bath."

"And what of it?" he grumbled. "It's not like I haven't seen it all before."

"Father!"

"Henry," their mother said soothingly. "That was years ago. When the girls were only children."

"I still think it's not right for a man to be denied access to his own home by his daughters," they heard him muttering outside. "What are they having a bath for anyway?"

"They're going to a dance, dear."

"A dance?" he scoffed. "Harriet, you know I frown upon such things. It's vulgar entertainment."

Increasingly nervous, Nettie and her two sisters listened to the unfolding argument. If Father was in a foul mood, he could be capable of forbidding them to go.

"Vulgar?" their mother countered. "Your drinking and gambling isn't that much better, dear Henry. Let the girls have their fun, I say. You've got yours."

"I see. Well, if it's like that, I'm off again. A man has to eat, and I came home in the hope of enjoying a good meal with my loving family. But I suppose I'll have to try my luck at The Boar's Head instead."

The three girls sighed with relief when they heard their father's voice trailing off as he left.

"Good riddance," Hannah said.

"I was worried Father would ruin our evening," Jane replied.

"Yeah, ruining other people's lives is his specialty."

"Hannah," Nettie admonished her sister. "You shouldn't say such things."

"It's true, isn't it?"

"Perhaps. But that still doesn't mean you should say these things out loud."

Nettie couldn't fault her sister. But as the eldest, she felt she had certain duties and responsibilities towards her siblings. Teaching them right from wrong was part of that.

"He's gone now," Jane said. "That's what matters." She smiled and continued, "Do you think there will be many nice boys at the dance?"

"That's what matters even more, isn't it?" Hannah teased.

Jane shrugged. "What's the point of going to a dance if there aren't any good-looking boys around?"

"Jane Morris!" Nettie said. "You forget yourself." But then she giggled. "Anyone in particular you're hoping to run into?"

Her youngest sister didn't answer.

"Look, she's blushing," Hannah laughed. "I bet she's thinking about Ben."

"Ben?" Nettie hadn't heard that name yet. But then again, at her sister's age, it seemed like she had a new admirer every month.

"He's the baker's youngest son," Hannah explained.

"His middle son, actually," Jane said. "And he happens to be very charming."

"I'm sure he is," Nettie smiled. "Just don't lose your head and don't do anything foolish, okay?"

"I would never," Jane replied earnestly, shocked her big sister would even mention the possibility.

The teasing, laughing and giggling continued while they got dressed and emptied the bathtub. When they were ready to leave for the dance, their mother stood waiting for them.

"You all look gorgeous," she beamed. "Have fun, but don't stay out too late, will you? We have another early start in the morning."

They nodded like three obedient and well-behaved daughters, and then the two youngest Morris sisters made a loud dash for the street.

Nettie wanted to set off too, but her mother stopped her. "You keep an eye on your sisters, Nettie dearest. You're the eldest and the wisest. Looking after them is your responsibility."

"I know, Mother."

"And I know you know, dear. I'm relying on you."

Nettie gave her mother a kiss on the cheek and then went to join her sisters, who were already out on the street waiting for her impatiently.

It would always be like this, wouldn't it? As the eldest of the three, she had a duty towards her two younger sisters. A family obligation. She loved Hannah and Jane dearly of course, and she would probably give her life for them if – heaven forbid – it ever came to that.

But it did make her wonder.

For how much longer would she need to shield and protect her sisters? She yearned for freedom. But the thought of leaving them behind with their father felt wrong.

They would find a husband at some point, get married and start a family of their own. Did that mean she had to postpone her own life until such time?

Even though the notion of marriage wasn't exactly uppermost in her mind, she didn't quite fancy the idea of becoming a spinster either.

Men have it so much easier, she sighed. *In so many matters.*

Chapter Seven

William kept an eye on his brothers, who were walking several yards in front of him, laughing and chatting each other's heads off. The three of them were on their way to The Black Swan, where they would meet up with a group of their cousins. Thomas and Joseph were excited about their night out, placing bets on who would get to dance with the most girls.

"I wager it's me," Thomas said. "I'll dance with at least ten different girls."

"I say William can do better," Joseph replied. "The girls like him more. You're too ugly."

"Ugly? All right then, little brother. I've got a penny here that says I'll dance with more girls than him."

"How many more?"

"Double the number. I'll dance with twice as many girls as William tonight."

"Deal," Joseph said, holding out his hand to his older brother to shake on their wager.

"Lads," William laughed, "I'm not sure how I feel about being the object of a bet. And I don't think the girls will be flattered if you dash from one to the next like a madman. That's not likely to make them feel special, you know."

"You're only saying that because you're afraid to lose," Thomas teased.

"Or maybe William has already got a particular girl in mind," Joseph chortled. "Someone you'd like to help feel special this evening, big brother?"

"Cheeky rascals," William smiled, as his brothers raced ahead again, hooting with laughter.

He loved being out with them like this. It was a chance to get away from their father and enjoy each other's companionship for a change. He didn't care much about the drinking, or even for the girls – although they were often a pleasant distraction. For him, simply spending some time off with his brothers was all the leisure he needed right now.

A shame they had to share that precious time with others, he thought. Especially if those others included their infamous cousin Robert.

The young man was as cruel and quick to anger as Father. And more worryingly, he always seemed to attract trouble.

"The Kirby boys!" Robert shouted when he spotted them coming. He and their other cousins were standing outside the alehouse. And it looked like they were already in a rowdy mood.

"Robert," William greeted him neutrally. Then he smiled and went through the usual round of shaking hands and patting shoulders with the others. His brothers were engrossed in discussing their plans with their younger cousins.

"How's my favourite uncle?" Robert asked.

"Father's fine."

"Of course he is. He always is. And you know why, William?"

"Tell me."

"Because Uncle George takes care of himself first."

He sure does, William thought with a sneer.

"Yup, Uncle George is an inspiration to me. You're lucky to have him as a father."

"Lucky," William repeated with more than a touch of sarcasm in his voice.

"What's wrong, Will? You sound gloomy."

William merely shrugged and looked for a way to tear himself away from Robert and talk to his other cousins instead. But Robert had a tendency to plant himself squarely in the centre of the group and dominate the conversation.

"I know what you need," Robert said cheerfully. "You need a good sip of this." Grinning, he held out a flask to William.

"What's that?"

"Drink it. You'll see."

Even as he brought the flask closer to his mouth, William could smell the alcohol inside. Cautiously, he took a small sip. The liquid scorched his throat and left a hot trail as it slid down to his belly.

"What the blooming heck is that?"

Robert laughed at his cousin's reaction. "My mother made it herself. Do you like it?"

Robert's mother, Aunt Martha, was their father's eldest sister. And her skill at distilling spirits made her rather popular within the family.

"Well, it's strong, that's for sure."

"Ha! Clever way of saying it doesn't agree with you, cousin. Maybe we should go inside and ask if they have some light cider for you."

The others laughed and Robert passed his flask around. "Make sure Thomas and Joseph get some too," he said.

Joseph politely refused, but Robert insisted.

"Everybody drinks tonight. That's the rule."

"Not if he doesn't want to," William replied. "The lad has come here to dance and have fun."

"Dance? That's a girls' thing. Men drink." Robert poked one of his cousins and added, "Real men, that is."

William rolled his eyes. The evening had barely started, but he was getting fed up with his annoying cousin already.

"Shall we go inside then?" he suggested.

"In there?" Robert pointed with his thumb at the alehouse behind them. "No, nothing but boring old men. Let's paint the town instead, I say." He turned to the group. "What about it, lads? Are you ready for some proper fun?"

Their inebriated cousins shouted their approval.

"Lead the way, Robert," someone laughed.

"Gladly," he said, with a fat wink at William and a stupid grin on his face.

Roaming the streets without any real aim or destination, their party grew increasingly louder while ale and Robert's nasty home-brew flowed copiously.

On several occasions, their cousin accosted complete strangers in the street. Trying to provoke people into an argument was his idea of fun. And the fact he had a band of drunken cousins behind him only added to his bold arrogance.

After an hour or so of this tedious parade, William had half a mind to say his goodbyes and take his brothers elsewhere.

But just then, Robert spotted another group of lads across the street. And a dangerously dark smirk appeared on his face.

"Well, well. Look who's there," he exclaimed, loud enough for the other young men to hear. "It's the onions and potatoes brigade!"

William vaguely recognised some of their faces. He had seen them at the market before and he understood they were all from costermonger families. He didn't really share his own family's hatred for these people. In his opinion, costers were only trying to make a living – just like anyone else.

But Robert was clearly of a different mind.

And so were the lads on the opposite side.

"Been digging through any good dustbins lately?" they shouted back. "We thought we could smell you filthy lot coming the moment we rounded the corner."

"We'd better be careful, lads," Robert mockingly warned his cousins. "They might be armed with – I don't know – rotting cabbages maybe."

"Getting one between your eyes might improve that hideous face of yours, ragman!"

"I'd like to see you try, coster!"

"Why don't you come over and we'll show you."

"No, why don't *you* come over here? Oh, I know why. It's because you're cowards, isn't it?"

"Say that again, rag boy," the leader of the rival group growled as he crossed the street.

William didn't see who threw the first clod of mud. But soon dirt, stones and all sorts of rubbish were flying through the air. Then, both groups stormed at each other and the clash began.

William had no intention of joining the fight, and he was mainly concerned about getting his brothers to safety. But since he was caught up in the street brawl, he didn't have much choice. Either he fought back, or he got his face smashed in. So he fought.

He mainly tried to fight his way to his brothers however. If he could get to them, he reasoned, the three of them might be able to run and escape from this stupid violence.

Suddenly, shouts and screams went up. "David! They've killed David!"

The fighting stopped and all eyes turned to Robert, who stood, with his fists still at the ready, above a fallen body. David, as the young man was called apparently, wasn't moving.

"No, he's just feigning it," Robert snarled. "Get up, you coward." Angrily, he kicked David in the gut.

But the young man didn't react at all.

"I'm telling you, he's dead," one of the costermonger boys said.

The shrill sound of a whistle startled everyone.

"It's the police," someone shouted. "Make yourselves scarce, lads!"

Both groups broke up and everyone scattered in different directions, while a handful of constables arrived at the scene. All they found was David's still body. Everyone else had fled.

William and his two brothers kept running until he was convinced nobody was following them and they were safe.

"Joseph, Thomas, are you boys all right?"

His brothers nodded, trying to catch their breath.

"Did you see that lad Robert knocked to the ground?" Joseph asked. "Do you think he was dead?"

"He wasn't moving much," Thomas said. "What's your guess, William? Did Robert kill him?"

"He's certainly mean and strong enough for it."

Joseph panicked. "What does that mean for us, William? Are we in trouble?"

"Well, if that costermonger lad is indeed dead..." He pursed his lips as he pondered the consequences.

"Then what? Say something, William!"

"Then that would make us witnesses to a crime. The police might even claim we were accomplices."

"Accomplices? What does that mean?

"It means they'll say we were to blame as well," Thomas explained. "And if that's the case, they'll probably lock us up too. Together with Robert."

Joseph gasped.

"Wait," William said, holding up his hands. "Stay calm, boys. First of all, we don't know if that lad is dead or not. But just to be on the safe side..."

He looked around, as if he was searching for something.

"What? What?!" Joseph insisted nervously.

"I think it would be best if we went somewhere busy. A place where lots of people can see us. That way, if the police come asking questions, we can say we weren't part of Robert's group. And we'll have plenty of eyewitnesses to confirm we were somewhere else."

"Sounds sensible enough," Thomas nodded. "So where do you suggest we go?"

William pointed at a public house down the road. The typical noise of merry revelry and music came drifting through its open door and windows.

"That sounds promising," he said. "Where there's music, there's bound to be people. Let's go."

Chapter Eight

Sitting on a bench at a table to rest her tired feet, Nettie laughed and clapped along to the rhythm of the music. Hannah and Jane were still dancing, mostly with each other. Nettie however wanted to sit this one out and take a breather. Watching her sisters and seeing the two girls enjoying themselves made her happy.

How wonderful it would be to feel this cheerful in all those other moments of their lives, she sighed. She didn't mind the hard work, the early mornings or the late nights. She could live with those. It was the constant worrying about money that bothered her. And she knew who was the main cause of those worries: her father and his never-ending stream of idiocy and big talk.

She shook her head. *Don't think about any of that now*, she told herself. She shouldn't let those thoughts ruin her evening. After all, she came here to have fun.

"You shouldn't be frowning like that, love," a man grinned at her. "It spoils that pretty little face of yours. Do you know what you need? Some good company, that's what."

"I'm fine, thank you," she said politely. From the look on his face and the smell of his breath, he was clearly drunk.

"Mind if I join you?"

"Yes, I do mind actually."

Completely ignoring her refusal, he lowered himself down next to her on the long wooden bench. "Oh, that feels good," he grunted. "All this dancing wears you out, doesn't it?"

He was sitting uncomfortably close to her, so Nettie shifted and slid away from him a bit more. But just as quick, he closed the gap between them again.

"Don't worry, love," he said. "I won't bite you. Not yet anyway, ha!" When he laughed, his rank breath wafted in her direction.

"Are you thirsty as well?" he asked, as he offered her the jug of ale he was carrying. "Here, have some of this."

"No, thank you. I should probably go and join my sisters again." She started to get up, but he grabbed her by the arm and pulled her back.

"Your sisters will be fine, love. Why don't you stay with me for a while longer?"

"I already told you no. Several times."

She tried to shake off his hand, but he only squeezed her arm harder.

"I insist," he growled. "What do you say you and I find ourselves a quieter spot, eh?"

Nettie wanted to lash out with her free hand. But he had anticipated that and grabbed her other arm as well.

"I like women with a bit of a fight in them," he smiled. Holding both her arms, he moved in to kiss her. Turning her head away, she barely managed to escape his lips.

"There you are," a friendly voice said. "I've been looking all over for you."

William smiled at her as if they were best friends.

"This place is so busy tonight, I thought I'd lost you in the crowd, dearest." He turned to the drunkard as if he had only now spotted the man. "This gentleman isn't bothering you, is he?"

The drunkard briefly eyed William up and down, weighed his options and then let go of Nettie. "I was just leaving," he grumbled.

Relieved, she let out a long breath when the man got up and disappeared into the crowd once more.

"Thank you," she said. "I was afraid I'd landed myself in a right pickle there."

"That's what it looked like from where I was standing too. Thought I'd better do something about it. I can't stand a drunkard, see."

"Alcohol does strange things to men," she nodded.

"For sure. My name is William by the way."

Nettie saw two teenage boys standing behind him. The youngest was tugging at his sleeve.

"And these are my two brothers," William said. "Thomas, and the little pest at my sleeve is Joseph."

"William," the youngest boy whispered urgently. "Don't you know who she is?"

Nettie smiled. "Pleased to meet you, William. And once again thank you. For your timely intervention."

He turned to his younger brothers. "Why don't you boys go and dance for a bit? You've still got that wager of yours going on, remember?"

"But William, she's—"

"Off you go then," he insisted, giving them a gentle shove towards where the people were dancing.

"What was that all about?" Nettie giggled.

"The wager? Nothing but a silly boys' affair. Mind if I sit down?"

She gestured at the bench, and with a polite nod he sat down next to her. At a more respectable distance, she was pleased to notice.

"Your brother seemed to be quite convinced he recognised me. Have we met before?"

William shrugged. "Not properly, no."

"And yet, you know me?"

"I wouldn't go so far as to claim I know you personally. But your father is a costermonger, isn't he? Mr Morris?"

"That's right." She was decidedly intrigued now. Who was this young man? "I'm Nettie Morris."

"Pleased to meet you, Miss Morris. As I said, I'm William. William Kirby."

Kirby? He was a ragman! And not just any old ragman either.

"Oh my," he laughed. "Judging by the look on your face, I'd say that penny must have dropped like lead."

She blushed, feeling slightly embarrassed about the fact her reaction had been so obvious to read.

"I'm sorry," she said. "I didn't mean to be rude."

"You weren't rude. It's no secret how our families feel about each other. Well, our fathers anyway."

"So why did you come over and save the daughter of your father's mortal enemy?"

"Mortal enemy? Blimey, that sounds grim, doesn't it?" He laughed and she thought it made him look even more friendly.

"But to answer your question, first of all, I hadn't recognised you yet when I saw that drunkard harassing you. And even if I had, I'd still have helped you. I can't tolerate men misbehaving towards women."

A good answer. But could she believe him?

"Spoken like a true gentleman," she smiled.

"I don't know about being a gentleman," he chuckled. "I'm just someone who appreciates good manners and a bit of kindness."

Fascinating. But she still hadn't decided if he was being truthful, or if he was merely speaking sweet words with an ulterior motive.

"A commendable attitude, Mr Kirby," she joked. "And one that makes you rather unusual round these parts, I should think."

He shrugged. "Someone has to set an example, I suppose. I'm doing it for my younger brothers' benefit as much as for anyone else, to be fair."

He nodded his head in the direction of the two lads who were having fun dancing. "I'd hate for them to take after their father too much."

"They seem friendly enough."

"Yeah, they're good lads, Thomas and Joseph."

"From the way you look at them, I can tell you care deeply for them."

"That's what big brothers do, isn't it?"

His words stirred an old pain inside her that she tried not to think of. She'd had an older brother once.

"Are you here on your own tonight?" he asked.

His question had sounded innocent, but it caused her to put her guard up instantly. Why did he want to know if she was alone?

"I'm here with my sisters," she replied, somewhat prudently.

"I'm sorry," he said quickly, registering her hesitant manner. "I didn't mean to intrude in your private affairs. It's just that we were talking about my brothers, so I merely wondered–"

"It's all right, Mr Kirby," she reassured him with a smile. "Perhaps it is me who should apologise to you. For overreacting again. I'm ashamed to admit my father's opinion about the Kirby family has affected me more than I would have thought."

"There's no need to apologise as far as I'm concerned, Miss Morris."

"But there is, Mr Kirby. It's not fair on you. You seem like a polite and perfectly decent young man."

"Tell you what. Let's start all over. Let's pretend my name isn't Kirby and yours isn't Morris." He paused for a heartbeat, before he added, "In fact, can I call you Nettie instead?"

She blushed.

For heaven's sake, Nettie. Get a hold of yourself.

Seeing her reaction, he started to stutter. "Perhaps that was too forward of me." He got up, ready to leave. "Forgive me, Miss Morris. I should not–"

"No, please. Stay."

She took a deep breath and straightened her shoulders. All this family rivalry was a load of nonsense, she decided. And if both she and him wanted to be different from their fathers, they might as well start to make their stand right there and then.

She looked at him and smiled kindly.

"Yes, you may call me Nettie... William."

Visibly relieved, he sat down again. The silence that fell over them was awkward and slightly tense. So he cleared his throat and asked, "Shall I get us something to drink? Some ale or cider?"

"I think after all this excitement, I should prefer to dance."

She held up her hand, as an open invitation to him. With a beaming smile on his face, he gladly took her hand and led her to the throng of people who were dancing to the merry tune of the lively music.

Chapter Nine

It was several hours later when Nettie and William emerged from the public house with their siblings in tow. The two of them had been dancing and talking with each other all night. Now, Nettie's head was spinning and she felt dizzy with delight.

"Thank you, William. I haven't had this much fun in ages."

"The pleasure was all mine, I assure you."

Nettie's sisters were standing a few steps away from her, while William's brothers were doing the same on the other side of the couple. Both groups were awkwardly trying not to stare at the others.

Feeling perfectly happy, Nettie sighed. She knew it was time to say their goodbyes, but she didn't want that to happen quite yet. When he took her hand, she gladly let him.

"Will I see you again?" he asked.

"Do you want to see me again?" she teased.

"Yes, I do."

She had to admit the look in his kind eyes seemed serious and sincere.

"Then you shall see me again. But you'll have to be smart about it."

"How so?"

She giggled. "Because I'm not sure how our fathers would feel about it."

"I know exactly how they'd feel about it," he chuckled. "They would absolutely hate it."

One more reason to continue seeing each other then, she thought.

"Don't worry though," he said. "I'll be very discreet."

"Thank you kindly, good sir," she quipped. "So you don't think keeping secrets from our fathers is bad?"

She meant it as a joke, but at the same time, she was curious to hear his response. Little things like that could tell you a great deal about a person's character.

He shrugged. "I don't really see it as keeping a secret from them. It's more like preventing unnecessary distress – for us and them."

"I think I know what you mean," she chuckled. Father didn't need to know. Not yet anyway.

First, she wanted to see where this would lead to. Whatever it was she and William had between them.

Because at the moment, they had merely spent a few hours in each other's company, dancing and chatting. But there was no denying they had been a very agreeable few hours.

"Anyway," he interrupted her thoughts. "It's late and I suppose we'd all better go home and get some sleep."

She nodded and slowly slipped her hand out of his. She thought he seemed equally reluctant to let go as she was.

"Shall I escort you home?" he asked. "I'd feel safer if you and your sisters didn't need to walk the streets alone this late at night."

"That's kind of you, but no, thank you. I'm sure we'll be fine. And I wouldn't want to risk any of the neighbours seeing us together."

"Fair enough. In that case, good night, Nettie."

"Good night, William."

They smiled at each other and then she turned around and started walking away with her sisters.

"He's still staring at you," Jane said when they were out of earshot.

"Is he now?" Nettie replied. She didn't want to look back herself, but knowing that he was still there brought a happy smile to her face.

"The two of you spent quite a lot of time together," Hannah said, in a way that made it clear she was fishing for more details.

"Yes, we did, didn't we?"

"Oh, stop teasing, Nettie! Who is he?"

"His name is William and he's a very nice young man. Charming and polite too." She paused, perfectly innocent, and then added, "And he's a Kirby."

Hannah and Jane gasped.

"A Kirby? Nettie! Father is going to be furious when he finds out."

"I know. And that's exactly why we won't be mentioning this little detail of our evening to him. Unless you would like him to keep us locked up indoors for the next three months?"

Hannah shook her head. "No, I'm okay with keeping my mouth shut."

"So what's this William like?" Jane asked. "Has he kissed you yet?"

"Jane Morris!" Nettie said, pretending to be shocked. "A lady shouldn't allow a man to kiss her that quickly."

The three girls giggled, the sound of their laughter echoing in the empty streets.

"That's a shame," someone growled as he grabbed Nettie and spun her around. It was the drunkard who had harassed her earlier. "Hello, love. Remember me?"

Jane and Hannah shrieked.

"Run, girls," Nettie told them. "Run!"

"But Nettie–"

"Don't worry about me. Run, I said!"

She threw her attacker a hard and defiant glare, while she listened to her sisters' fleeing footsteps. The man grinned drunkenly at her.

"That's very noble of you, my darling. To be so concerned about the safety of your sisters."

"What do you want?" Nettie asked, not showing him any trace of fear.

"What do you think?" he laughed. "Let's start with that kiss you denied me."

He leaned forward to kiss her lips, but she turned away and raised her arms to keep him away. Yet, the more she struggled, the more he tightened his grip.

"Nobody refuses me, love. That's a lesson I'll teach you soon enough."

"Here's a lesson for you, good man," William's voice suddenly sounded from behind them as he pulled the drunkard away from Nettie. "Stop bothering women."

Before the attacker could react, William planted a fist right between the man's eyes. Dizzy and drunk, the assailant took a few stumbling steps.

"I'll make you regret that, you worm," he grunted when he had regained his footing.

"No, you won't," William replied confidently. "I suggest you walk away and disappear. Now."

The man lashed out and tried to hit William. But all the alcohol had made his movements slow, and his aim poor. So William had no trouble blocking the punch. In response, he drove his own fist into the soft underbelly of his opponent, making the man double over.

It took a few more of his futile attempts before the drunkard understood he was no match for William. With one last dark look at Nettie, he stumbled away, muttering to himself.

"Are you all right?" William asked her while he kept one eye on the retreating figure. "Did he hurt you?"

"No, I'm fine. Thank you. That's the second time you've saved me this evening."

He took her hands and gave them a reassuring squeeze. "I hope we won't always meet under these special circumstances."

"What made you come back?"

"Once you'd gone, I kept worrying about you. Had this feeling in my gut. So I told my brothers to go home without me and turned back. It seems I got here just in time."

"Nettie!" her sisters shouted as they came running back. "Thank heavens you're safe."

"Thanks to William," she replied.

"Thank you, Mr Kirby," Hannah said.

"Yes, thank you, Mr Kirby," Jane echoed sweetly. "Nettie was right when she said you were a nice young man."

"My pleasure," he laughed. "This time however, I insist on walking the three of you home. Just tell me when we're almost there and

I'll turn back before we come into sight of your house. Fair?"

"Fair," Nettie nodded, slipping her hand into the crook of his arm. She realised it was only now that her heart started to calm down after being frightened from the assault.

They walked in silence, relieved that a nasty incident had been averted. Nettie felt grateful for having William by her side. She thought she might want to have him around more often.

"Girls," she told her sisters. "Now we really must keep this between us. If Father hears about everything that happened this evening, he will never let us out of the house again." She looked over at William. "And we don't want that, do we?"

"My lips are sealed," Hannah said.

"Sister's honour," Jane giggled.

Chapter Ten

Grateful for its warmth, Nettie blew on the cup of tea she was holding between her hands. The scent of the strong brew came whirling up softly into her nostrils, helping to revive her tired spirits. The morning air outside was chilly, and the costermonger families huddled close together in small groups while they waited for the wholesalers to open.

As always, the nearby coffee stall was doing good business from them, selling toasted and buttered bread and hot drinks to the small yet hungry crowd. Someone was passing a flask around, to add a little something stronger to their tea or coffee, as he put it. His offer was gratefully accepted by most.

You had to be early if you wanted the best choice of produce, which meant getting up before dawn. Normally, Nettie didn't mind too much – she was used to these hours by now. But on a morning like today, after such an eventful evening, it just took a bit longer for her mind to wake up and work at its usual pace.

Carefully, she sipped her tea. As the hot liquid made its way down her throat, she closed her eyes so she could enjoy the sensation more.

"That looks like it hit the right spot," her friend Anne said with a smile. "So I take it you've had a lovely evening then?"

Nettie merely nodded and made a noise that was supposed to be a confirmation. She glanced at her sisters, who were both with her – equally tired and cold. The expression on their faces told her they hadn't forgotten about their agreement.

"And did you meet anyone interesting?" Anne prodded.

"You know how it is with these dances. Some people are nicer than others."

She wasn't planning on sharing the news about William with Anne. The girl was a good friend, but also a terrible gossip who couldn't keep a secret if her life depended on it.

"What about you, Jane?" Anne asked, trying her luck with the younger girl. "Did you get to dance with lots of boys?"

"A few," Jane replied, visibly wary of saying anything that might get them into trouble.

But Anne picked up on that as well. "You lot are being strangely evasive this morning," she said. "What happened? Come on, tell me."

"We're just a bit tired, Anne. That's all."

"Hmph, I still say you're hiding something from me. Never mind. I'm bound to find out sooner or later." She giggled.

Nettie took another sip from her tea, so she wouldn't need to respond to her friend's obvious attempt to elicit more information from her.

"Have you heard the big news yet?" Anne asked. "Your cousin David nearly got killed last night."

"David? What happened?"

He was the eldest son of one of her aunts. They didn't see him very often, mostly because Mother didn't particularly like her husband's sisters. A sentiment which Nettie shared. They were a quarrelsome bunch, her aunts. And whenever they got together with her father, who was their only brother, they would talk and bicker so much and so loudly, it gave her a splitting headache.

"They say he was attacked by a vicious gang – mostly ragmen of course," Anne explained. "He was out on the street with some of his friends, minding their own business, when suddenly those dirty good-for-nothings showed up and jumped on the poor lads. Ended up nearly killing your cousin, they did!"

"That sounds awful. Do they know who did it?"

"I told you, ragmen. They made no secret of who they were, those lice-ridden, arrogant louts."

Ignoring Anne's inflammatory tone, Nettie asked, "And you said David nearly got killed?"

"They beat him so badly, for a while the police thought he wouldn't make it."

"So the police are involved, are they?"

"They broke up the fight and found your cousin lying on the street, unconscious. But you know what the police are like. They don't care about us."

"But if David's friends saw who did it, they should tell them. Then the police can arrest the culprits."

Anne snorted. "Nettie, listen to yourself. As if the police would bother. I'm told your aunt had to beg them not to fine David for being involved in the fight. Tell you what though, I think your father is in a righteous state."

Following the direction in which Anne inclined her head, Nettie looked over at where her father was standing, several yards away.

Henry Morris had managed to claim the spot he loved most: in the very centre of attention. And from the sound of it, he was upset alright. Which wasn't all that unusual for him of course. Loudly proclaiming his dismay at this or that was a regular routine of his. But having just heard the news about her cousin, Nettie understood what her father's anger would be about this morning.

"A disgrace," he declared in that deep and loud voice of his, hardened by years of working at the market. "That's what this is. A complete and utter disgrace. That poor lad could have died at the cruel hands of those wretched ragmen. And what will the police do about it?"

"Nothing at all," someone muttered. "As always."

"Exactly. The police won't lift a finger. It's as if our lives don't matter. Do you know what we should do?"

"No, but I'm sure you're going to tell us, Henry," a man sniggered. Nettie's father was so caught up in his own passion however, that he didn't notice the mocking tone.

"We should seek out the people who did this and teach them a lesson. Show them what the costers are made of." He held up his arm and shook an angry fist at an invisible adversary. "That way, they might learn to respect us some more."

A few people started nodding and mumbling in agreement. Nettie's father revelled in the attention he was getting.

"To the young men among you, I ask: will you stand idly by? Will you let this vile and humiliating deed go unpunished? If we allow these savages to get away with crimes like this, you could be their next victim." He wagged an ominous finger above his head. "Heed my words, I tell thee. Heed my words!"

"You should have been a preacher, Henry," someone laughed. "Maybe Father Michael could use your help."

"Mr Morris is right," one of the young lads in the crowd shouted. "We should do something about this insult!"

Over on their side, Nettie shook her head. "Nothing good can come from all this agitated nonsense. If they don't calm down, people are going to end up doing something rash."

She knew her father well enough to understand his little improvised speech was mainly a load of bombastic posturing and bluff – designed to draw attention and gain the approval of others. But she was worried about what might happen if people took his words seriously.

"Your father really should have been a preacher," Anne giggled.

"Hmm, I don't think so. Priests are supposed to spread a message of love and forgiveness. Not hate and vengeance."

"Forgiveness? But what about your cousin? Don't you feel it was bad what those ragmen did to him?"

"Of course it was wrong! I absolutely abhor senseless violence. No matter who's committing it." She sighed. "I honestly don't see why anyone would intentionally get into a fight."

"That's men for you, I suppose. They do it for fun."

"I could never love a man like that. Someone who spends their evenings drinking and fighting? Not for me, thank you very much."

"Speaking of men and evening entertainment," Anne said. "Are you going to tell me about last night or not?"

"What's there to tell?"

"Oh, don't pretend nothing happened, Nettie. Your eyes betray you."

Nettie concentrated on her cup of tea and tried not to blush.

"See?" Anne squealed. "I knew it! You met a boy, didn't you? Ooh, he must be special if he took your fancy."

"Perhaps," she grinned.

Chapter Eleven

Sitting at a small table in The Black Swan with his two brothers, William eagerly tucked into his plate of bacon and eggs. Chewing with his mouth full, he tore off a piece of bread and spread some butter on it.

"That's quite an appetite you've got there, big brother," Thomas grinned. "Last night seems to have made you hungry."

"A man's got to keep his energy up, doesn't he?" William replied with a grin.

"For sure," Thomas nodded. "So did you expend a lot of your energy then?" He winked at their younger brother and gave him a playful nudge with his elbow. Joseph snorted with laughter and covered his mouth.

"You could call it that, I suppose," William said. "Last night was... eventful, to say the least."

"I bet it was! And those events wouldn't happen to involve a certain young lady, would they?"

"They did indeed," William smiled, before drinking a sip of coffee.

"Oh-ho, you cheeky rascal! Care to share any details?"

"Lads, it's not what you think. Remember I told you boys to walk home without me? Because I had a bad feeling? Turns out I was right. I got back to her just in time to drag that drunkard off of her."

"Always the gentleman. I'm sure she was very grateful to you."

"She was. Then I walked her home with her sisters, and that was it."

Thomas glanced over his shoulder and lowered his voice. "You *did* realise who she was, didn't you?"

"A lovely young woman, you mean?"

"Come on, Will. Don't play the fool with me."

William grinned. "If you're talking about her family, then yes, I know what they do for a living. So what of it?"

His brother shrugged. "Nothing, I suppose. She seemed like a nice girl, I'll admit that."

"I'm not sure Father would agree though," Joseph whispered.

"Nothing William does will ever agree with Father," Thomas sneered.

"Quite," William said. "So let's not tell him just yet, shall we? Speaking of whom–" He looked over his shoulder to where their father was talking excitedly to a group of other men. "He seems to be in an unusually good mood this morning. Anybody happen to know why?"

"Last night's street fight," Thomas replied.

"That's made him happy, has it? Typical."

Suddenly, wild roars of cheer and praise went up among their father's party when the pub door opened and cousin Robert walked in.

"There he is," George Kirby shouted proudly. "The hero who stood up for the honour of the ragmen!"

Over at their table, William rolled his eyes.

"Thank you, Uncle," Robert said, smiling modestly. "It was no great deal really."

"No great deal? Nonsense, lad! You sure showed those vegetable mongers. Taught them the difference between a man and a limp turnip, you did."

He shook Robert's hand and pulled him into the middle of the group. Men clapped him on the shoulder, as if he was a prize-winning champion.

"It's a shame the miserable oaf isn't dead," William's father said. "Now that would really have taught them a lesson."

"He came close to dying from what I've heard," Robert smirked. "And I didn't even hit him all that hard. Imagine the damage I could have done if I had tried."

"Of course you would have. What with those fine fists of iron of yours." George Kirby raised his own fists like a boxer and exchanged a few mock punches with Robert, who happily played along.

Laughing, he threw his arms around his favoured nephew and gave him a manly hug.

"Your mother must be very proud of you," he said. "I wish my own sons were more like you." He looked over at William. "If they were half the man you are, I'd be pleased."

"Don't be too hard on them, Uncle. Your boys were there as well last night."

"They were? Well, they certainly didn't tell me about it. I don't suppose they were any good? Or perhaps they ran at the first sight of trouble?"

"I don't know to be honest. I didn't see. Too busy hitting costermonger boys in their ugly faces."

The group of men roared with raw and malicious laughter. Someone handed Robert a mug of ale, which he gratefully accepted and immediately placed at his lips.

"Tell you what though," William's father said. "I would love to see those ugly faces this morning. I wonder what I'd enjoy seeing more: their bruises or the shame of their defeat."

"Why don't you go and find out, George?" someone suggested jokingly.

"Perhaps I should. You know, just to rub it in a bit more. Cut those milk-livered maggots down to size." He emptied his beer and wiped his mouth with the back of his hand. "Aye, that's what I'll do."

He held up his empty beer mug at the landlord to indicate he wanted another one.

"Boys," he called over to his sons. "As soon as I've finished my breakfast here, we'll swing by the market where those costers usually peddle their muck."

"Do you think that's wise, Father?" William asked.

"Wise? Who cares if it's wise or not." He took the fresh mug of beer that the landlord handed him and went over to his son's table.

"Only grey old men with weak backs care about wisdom," he scowled. "Or cowards who are looking for an excuse not to act." He took a big swig of his beer. "Maybe it's time you grew a pair, son."

"I assure you there's nothing wrong with the pair I already have, Father," William replied defiantly.

With his breath reeking of beer, his father bent forwards so his head was close to William's face. In a low and menacing voice, he growled, "You'll soon get a chance to prove that, I'm sure. Then we'll see what sort of a man you really are."

William didn't blink an eye and stared at his father without a hint of fear. George Kirby merely grinned and returned to his friends, where everyone continued to talk and boast loudly.

"Do you think Father meant what he said?" Joseph asked timidly.

William shrugged and ate the last of his bacon. Inside, he was seething at his father. But he felt it was important to put on an air of calm indifference – for the sake of his brothers. He wanted them to know he wasn't impressed by any of their father's words. And he hoped that they too would learn not to be intimidated by a bully.

"He sounded serious enough," he said, mopping up his plate with a piece of bread. "I happen to think that going to the market on purpose to taunt those people would be needlessly foolish. But then again, that's exactly the sort of thing Father would do." He popped the bread in his mouth and sighed.

"But what if anyone recognises us, William?"

He could see his youngest brother was worried.

"Who knows," Thomas scoffed. "Maybe that's what Father is hoping for. He loves a bit of trouble, he does."

"It's a distinct possibility. So I suggest we let him do all the talking, while we keep quiet in the background. Besides, by the time we get there, he'll probably be too drunk to notice us."

"The way he's been drinking," Thomas snorted, "I'd say there's a good chance he'll fall asleep on top of our cart before we get to the market."

He did a convincing impression of a drunken man snoring with his tongue hanging out of his mouth, which made his brothers laugh.

"Relax, Joseph," William said, seeing the worried expression on his youngest brother's face. "Father's bark is worse than his bite."

Although the man's bite did hurt, he thought to himself, remembering the numerous occasions when he had felt the wrong side of his father's hand or belt.

But maybe there was a way to keep his brothers out of harm's way, William considered.

"Here's an idea. Why don't you go searching around for rags and useful things, while I stay with Father? There's no use in all three of us tagging along with him."

No use in exposing you to whatever trouble Father is bound to get us into either, he added silently.

Chapter Twelve

Much to Nettie's despair, business was slow at the market that morning. Despite the fact they had managed to claim a favourable spot, on a corner that got plenty of foot traffic, customers just didn't appear to be buying much. People seemed interested, keenly inspecting all the fresh vegetables and fruit the Morris family had on offer. But they weren't parting with their coins as readily as most other mornings.

At first, Nettie thought she was merely imagining it. But a quick inspection of the money in the large pocket of her apron showed that her impression was correct.

And she wasn't the only one to notice.

"It's because of Father," Hannah grumbled quietly to Nettie. "He's still in one of his funny moods because of that sorry business with David last night. And it's scaring people off."

"Oh, come now, Hannah," she replied. "I'm sure it's not that bad." Although, if she had to be honest about it, she wasn't too convinced by her own words.

"I'm telling you, it's true," her sister insisted. "Just observe him for a while and you'll see I'm right. He seems annoyed, and he's trying too hard. People pick up on that somehow. Nobody likes it when you push for the sale."

"I guess that means we'll have to smile twice as nice at people," Nettie said as she gave her sister's arm a supportive squeeze. "That way, maybe they'll ignore the grumpy old goat."

Hannah sighed. "I suppose you're right." She shook her head and giggled. "Grumpy old goat, I like that one. That's exactly what he is at the moment, isn't he?"

Jane came tugging at Nettie's sleeve. "Don't look now, but isn't that... you know... *him*? The boy you met last night?"

Casually, Nettie glanced in the direction her youngest sister was indicating with a nod of the head. Her heart skipped a beat when she saw William approaching. He was pushing a cart piled high with all sorts of rags and clothes, while old pots and pans dangled on the sides.

Walking next to him – or rather, stumbling along drunkenly – was a man who she assumed was his father. She vaguely remembered her father pointing Mr Kirby out to her, many years ago when she was only a child. And she certainly recognised some of William's features in him.

Although William looked much softer and nicer.

Holding her breath, she looked at her father. He hadn't seen his nemesis yet, but she knew that would change soon enough. Because it was clear where William and his father were heading: straight their way.

"Put her over there, son," George Kirby said, pointing at a space directly opposite the Morris stall. "That's as good a spot as any."

Nettie's father's nostrils flared when he saw the two men setting down their cart. Placing his fists on his hips, he glared angrily at the ragman he hated so much. But before he got a chance to say anything, Mr Kirby started calling out to the crowd.

"I've got everything you need, fine sirs and madams! Whether it's a pair of shoes for your feet, a hat to cover your precious head, or a pan to boil your eggs in the morning – you'll find it right here."

With an artful flourish, he doffed his cap at a portly looking matron. "Good morning to you, my beautiful. Fancy treating yourself to a shawl to grace those lovely shoulders of yours?"

As if he was a magician, he pulled a scarf from the pile of rags on his cart and draped it over the matron's shoulder.

"Just look how that colour suits you, dear. And because today is a special day, I'll make you a good price too. A special price for a special lady."

Charmed by his flattering ways, the matron chuckled, "What's so special about today then, you saucy rascal?"

"Let's just say I have something to celebrate this morning." He made a point of staring at Nettie's father with a broad grin on his face. "Something to be very happy about."

The matron giggled, but then she moved on.

"Did you hear that, Henry?" the man from the stall next to theirs said. "Not hard to tell why that cheeky sod is so cheerful, eh?"

"He's got some nerve coming here, parading and gloating right underneath our noses," Nettie's father replied.

When he stomped over to Mr Kirby's cart, Nettie groaned silently. *This is how the trouble starts.*

"Say, you," her father called out sternly. "Don't you know you need a license to trade at this market?"

"But I'm not trading," William's father grinned. "I'm merely stopping by. Resting my poor back. And if in the meantime someone sees anything useful on my cart and they want to buy it?" He shrugged his shoulders. "Who am I to stop them?"

"That's trading, you dimwitted barnacle!"

"Who are you calling a barnacle, you bloated pignut?"

Nettie squirmed at their loud exchange of insults. Business was slow enough without these two fighting cocks having an argument in public. Already, a small crowd was gathering to gawk at the bickering duo.

Glancing over at William, she noticed he was keeping his distance from his father and doing his best to look the other way. When their eyes met briefly, he smiled at her. But he also seemed embarrassed to be there. She gathered he probably shared her feelings about their fathers' behaviour.

By now the two men were, quite literally, in each other's faces. Their chests and bellies were touching, each man standing his ground and willing the other to step away.

"We all know why you're really here," Nettie's father said.

"Well, it's certainly not to enjoy the view. Because I have to say, my view's pretty ugly at the moment."

"Gentlemen, please," the voice of Father Michael pleaded. The priest came rushing towards the scene, intent on preventing the situation from escalating. "Let's not have any unpleasantness in a public space such as this one."

Smiling amicably, he placed a gentle hand on each man's shoulder. Both men took a reluctant step back, but kept eyeing each other angrily.

"Surely you are here to trade, and not to argue," Father Michael spoke soothingly.

"He's the one who started it, Father," Henry Morris said, pointing at his adversary. "That miserable fleabag came here to gloat at us."

"You're the one who stepped up to me and started calling me names, cabbage face."

"Gentlemen, please! I don't think this sort of language is necessary or helpful. And I must ask you to remember your positions. You are both well-known and respected members of our community. People turn to you for guidance and they expect you to set an example."

Nettie thought that was a rather blatant attempt at flattery from Father Michael. But it also seemed to have the desired effect. Both her father and Mr Kirby calmed down a little and turned up their noses at each other.

"Now, I understand there's been a violent confrontation between several young men last night. And I can see why that would upset your feelings. But–"

"It's done more than upset some feelings, Father! That band of thugs nearly killed my poor nephew. And I'm sure this scoundrel here knows all about it."

Nettie's father thumped Mr Kirby in the chest with his finger. That triggered the latter into a furious reaction, but Father Michael quickly positioned himself in between the two men to keep them apart.

"Enough," he commanded. "One tragic incident will suffice. There's no need to shed any more blood, don't you think?"

Mr Kirby shrugged and grinned, "They bleed easily, these turnip mongers."

"Did you hear that, Father? He's as guilty as sin, I tell you!"

"Gentlemen, for the last time! I must insist that you cease this senseless bickering. You are causing a scene and your fellow tradesmen are losing business because of it."

Nettie's father and Mr Kirby straightened their clothes, each man's arrogant glare accusing the other one of being responsible for the spectacle they both made of themselves.

"You're right, Father," Henry Morris said. "It was unwise of me to lower myself to other people's uncivilised level."

"And I was leaving anyway," George Kirby said. "I don't like the look of certain characters at this market. A bit too full of themselves for my taste."

Father Michael looked warily from one man to the other, as they both turned their backs to each other.

"Let's go, son," Mr Kirby said, walking past their handcart.

William took hold of the two-wheeled cart, but before he started pulling it, he stole one last glance at Nettie. They smiled at each other, and then she quickly turned her head away. Not because she didn't want to look at him, but because she was afraid her father would notice.

The morning had already been eventful enough as it was, and she didn't want to add any further complications. Even more so since she wasn't entirely sure yet how she felt about William.

She had liked the time they had spent together last night. But now she reminded herself of what she always told her sisters: don't lose your head and don't do anything foolish.

Following her own advice would be the sensible thing to do. No matter how sweet and charming William Kirby seemed to be.

Chapter Thirteen

Her father was restless for the remainder of the morning. Normally, he wouldn't stop talking – either with their customers, random passers-by or the other market people. He'd talk about anything from the weather to the rising cost of living, and he always seemed to be abreast with everyone's family events.

But not today. This morning, he was unusually quiet. And when he did speak, he sounded as if his heart wasn't in it. Instead, he paced up and down a lot, while he wrung his hands nervously.

Nettie rather suspected it was because of the incident with William's father earlier. And she guessed what his solution for his discomfort would be.

So when he came sidling up to her shortly after the church bells had struck twelve, Nettie already knew what he was going to say.

"Nettie dearest, I'm afraid all that commotion has adversely affected my good-natured disposition."

"I'd noticed as much, Father."

"Ah, see! You've noticed it too, have you? That's what that filthy ragman will do to an honest man, you know. Destroy my income and my business, it would. I think I need to unwind for a while. Take my mind off this sad and sorry affair."

She knew that meant he would be off to the alehouse for the rest of the day.

"That's fine, Father. Hannah and I can manage."

"Are you sure?"

As if he would change his mind if she said no.

Jane and Mother were off delivering orders, and it was possible that she and her sister would get rather busy running the stall on their own. But he hadn't exactly been much use to them this morning, more of a hindrance. So having him out of their way might actually prove more helpful.

"I shan't be too long," he said, which she knew to be a lie. Casting aside any feeling of shame or guilt, he then added, "In the meantime, Nettie, try to sell some of our pots and pans, will you? I've invested so much money in them, and the least you could do is put a bit more effort into selling them."

"What?!"

"There's no need to act insulted, girl. I'm merely asking you to try a little harder." He picked up one of their shiny new pots and admired it. "They're of such fine quality, but we're not selling any and I need to start repaying the money I borrowed. So put your best foot forward and all that."

Nettie couldn't believe he was blaming her for the fact his stupid idea wasn't working out – just like she had predicted. But she decided against mentioning that to him. The sooner he was out of her sight, the better.

"Well, toodle-pip," he said cheerfully as he set the pot down again.

Of all the nerve, she grumbled to herself while she watched him stroll away, whistling a carefree tune.

Still, she preferred it this way. Because as much as she resented her father for leaving them to carry the burden while he went off drinking, she was also grateful to have some time to think. With everything that had happened since the previous evening, she felt she needed to sort her mind out.

At first, meeting William had just seemed like a pleasant encounter. He had been someone to talk to and share a laugh with for a few hours. Now however, she was surprised to discover she couldn't stop thinking about him.

She hadn't minded the fact he belonged to the family her father loved to hate. But that street fight was stirring up the old hatred. So this wasn't a good time for their fathers to find out she and William had met each other at the dance.

Nettie sighed. *Oh, these foolish men with their foolish fights.* Trying to make a living was hard enough. Why did they have to waste their energy on senseless feuds? She was glad William hadn't got involved in the argument earlier. Maybe it showed he wasn't like those other men, she thought.

Her sister made her snap out of her musings with a nudge of the elbow. "Look who's there,"

Hannah said, nodding her head in a direction to the right of them.

It was William, and he seemed to be walking towards them, smiling broadly as he spotted her. She loved to see that smile of his.

"Hello there," she said when he came up to her.

"Hello, Nettie. Nice to see you again."

She nodded and then she averted her eyes to try and stop herself from blushing.

"I wanted to drop by and apologise for my father's behaviour this morning."

"That's very kind of you. But I don't think you should be apologising on your father's behalf."

"Perhaps not. But still, I'm sorry you had to witness that ridiculous scene."

"It was a bit ridiculous, wasn't it?" she giggled.

"Yeah, I swear my father and yours looked like two bloated toads puffing themselves up to get the better of each other."

"That's a very accurate description," she laughed. "Anyway, I'm glad you came by. And you chose the right time too. Toad number two has just left for the pub."

"Toad number one was busy haggling over a load of old rags with a trader when I slipped away. I'm sure he's spending all our profit on beer as well by now. Fathers, eh?"

They exchanged a knowing smile and then a silence settled between them while they looked each other in the eye.

He was the first to break eye contact this time, pretending to look at their new pots and pans.

"These are really nice," he said. "Unusual for a fruit and vegetable monger to be selling pots and pans. But very nice nonetheless."

"One of my father's brilliant plans, I'm afraid. He's always coming up with these daft ideas to make more money, thinking he's clever. But most of them fail miserably. These pots and pans are no different. He's had to borrow money to purchase them, but so far we haven't sold a single one of them." She rolled her eyes. "And obviously, that's because I'm not trying hard enough."

"It sounds like our fathers have more in common than they would care to know," William chuckled. "Mine is like that as well. Obsessed with squeezing every last penny out of any opportunity he sees. And when his schemes don't work, he always finds someone else to blame for his failures."

"It would be funny if it weren't so sad, I suppose."

He shrugged. "You can't teach an old fox new tricks. I've given up any hope of my father ever changing his ways. I'm mostly biding my time until I've saved up enough money so I can leave and strike out on my own."

"Ah, so you're an ambitious man," she quipped.

"If you want to call it that. Personally, I like to think of it more as having a goal in life. What about you, Nettie? Have you got any dreams?"

"Of course I do. But I've also got two younger sisters to worry about."

"I know what you mean. I've got two brothers myself. But the way I see it, they have their own life to live and their own choices to make. And at some point, they'll need to stand on their own two feet."

"That's true, I guess," she nodded. Although she knew perfectly well she was far from ready to let go of her sisters and leave Hannah and Jane behind with their father.

"Anyway, listen to us being two boringly responsible adults," he joked as he knocked against the side of a big pan with one of his knuckles. "I came here to say hello to you and somehow we seemed to have ended up discussing future plans."

"Conversations can be like that sometimes." She didn't mind talking about the future with him.

"Speaking of plans," he grinned, "what are you doing on Sunday?"

Cheeky, she thought, while at the same time liking him for it. But before she could answer his question, an angry shout went up.

"That's one of them," a young man cried. Standing with a handful of his friends, he pointed at William.

Chapter Fourteen

The youths came running over. Nettie recognised them. They were all sons of other costermongers at the market. And they seemed infuriated. William tensed up as they stood in a half circle in front of him, blocking any means of escape. The menacing tension between them was so thick, Nettie could feel it hanging in the air.

"Look who we have here," the leader of the small group growled at William.

"Charlie, what's this about?" Nettie asked him in a tone that made it clear she was none too pleased with this turn of events.

"Stay out of this, Nettie. This is men's business."

"I think I've had my fill of men's business this morning, thank you very much. I don't want any more trouble, do you hear?"

"Like I said, Nettie, this doesn't concern you."

"If you're going to be threatening people and scaring away my customers, then it does concern me."

The argument between her father and Mr Kirby had been bad enough. She was in no mood for a repeat performance. Two public squabbles in the same day, that's how a bad reputation got started.

But the leader of the group decided to ignore her and turned to William instead. "Did you honestly think we wouldn't recognise you?"

"I didn't realise I was famous," William grinned. "I don't believe we've met."

"Did you hear that, lads?" Charlie smirked at his friends. "The gentleman believes he hasn't made our acquaintance yet." He turned back to William and narrowed his eyes. "Yes, we've met before alright, you filthy ragman. Just last night in fact. When you and your friends tried to kill David."

"I don't know what you're talking about."

"Ha! I knew ragmen weren't smart, but you must be particularly stupid if you've forgotten already. Let me refresh your memory. You were part of the group who attacked us. I distinctly remember seeing your ugly face."

"Is that so?" William sneered.

Charlie nodded and stepped right up to him. "I didn't see who was responsible for knocking David unconscious. But for all we know, it was you."

"Or maybe you didn't see me there at all and you're only saying that because you don't like my kind."

"You're right about one thing, ragman. I don't like your kind. And I like you even less after what you did to David last night."

"Tell you what *I* don't like," William said. "I don't like having people this close to my face." With a sudden shove, he sent Charlie stumbling back into the arms of the young man's friends.

His eyes wide with shock and his nostrils flaring in anger, Charlie seethed, "Don't you dare touch me again, ragman."

"Then don't stand so close to me, coster."

"Boys!" Nettie shouted. "I've had more than enough of this nonsense. If it's a fight you want, then I suggest you take it elsewhere. This is a market, not a pub. I've got a business to run here."

"I'm sorry, Nettie," Charlie said. "But this filthy dog has no right to show his face around here."

"He's got as much right to come to the market as anyone else. But if you insist on continuing to make a scene like this, I'm going to have to ask you to leave. Now."

She looked around, desperately wishing Father Michael would show up again to calm things down. But unfortunately, the priest was nowhere to be seen this time.

"Nettie, this piece of ragman filth helped his friends to beat up your cousin! Doesn't that bother you?"

"Any form of violence bothers me. And that includes what's going on right in front of me here. So I want you all to stop this stupid bickering."

"Bickering? Nettie, this is a serious matter. He attacked us and nearly killed David!"

"You keep saying that, Charlie. But what makes you so sure it was him?"

"Because I saw him with my own two eyes!"

"And what time was this? Was it after dark?"

"Yes, it was after dark. But I could still make out their faces. Why are you defending this filthy dog anyway, Nettie?"

"He's got a name, Charlie. And I'm not defending anyone. All I'm saying is maybe William wasn't there last night."

"Of course he was. I saw him, didn't I?" A look of suspicion came over his face. "How do you know his name?"

Nettie rolled her eyes. These idiot men with their ridiculous games. But if she told him William had spent the evening with her, she'd probably get in trouble.

Perhaps I should just tell him though. At least that would end this stupid argument.

She opened her mouth to blurt it out, but William raised his hand and stopped her short.

"Don't waste your breath on this fool, Miss Morris," he said. "You'd stand a better chance trying to convince a brick wall."

"Did you just call me a fool, you dirty rat?"

"I did. Only a fool would continue to argue after the young lady asked us not to because it's hurting her business."

"Clever with words, are you? All right then. Let's take this argument elsewhere. Like the young lady requested." He took a step closer to William, his eyes dark with menace.

"There is no argument as far as I'm concerned." William sounded unimpressed by Charlie's threats. "I came here to have a friendly conversation. And I don't remember inviting you to it."

"You talk like a coward. How about we see if you can fight like a man?"

"I don't want to fight. Not with you or anyone else."

"What if we made you?" Charlie asked as he suddenly made a grab for the collar of William's shirt.

Having anticipated the move, William easily swatted Charlie's hand away. And just as quickly, he retaliated by punching his opponent in the gut. Using the short moment of confusion to his advantage, he decided to make his escape. But not before turning to Nettie and giving her a wink.

"Have to run. Bye!"

Howling with rage, Charlie and his friends chased after him through the crowd.

"Stop, you hooligans," Nettie shouted. "Leave him alone!"

But they were already out of earshot. And even if they had heard her, she was under no illusion that they would have listened to her.

"What was that all about?" Hannah asked, appearing by her sister's side.

"A bunch of lads claimed William was involved in that fight last night."

"William? But he was with you all night."

Nettie shrugged. "Charlie was adamant they saw him with the group they ran into."

"Strange. Do you believe him?"

"To be honest, I don't know who to believe."

The exchange had left her confused. She wanted to believe William. Mainly because she liked him a lot more than Charlie. But she also realised she hardly knew anything about him. He was someone she had met only yesterday.

Funny, she smiled to herself. Had it really been yesterday? Already, it felt like she knew him far longer. They got along so nicely.

Part of her was eager to find out the truth of the matter. Who was right and who was wrong? But then again, perhaps not knowing was the better option.

"Well, whatever happened last night," Hannah said, "I hope William will be all right. Those boys seemed mad like hell the way they went after him."

Nettie nodded and bit her lip. She had to admit that worried her too. In fact, she found herself worrying more for his safety than about the truth of the incident.

She would hate to see William getting hurt at the hands of Charlie and his friends. No matter what his involvement might have been.

Chapter Fifteen

"Nettie, wake up," Hannah whispered as she softly shook her older sister. "We're running late."

Nettie felt like she had to drag herself up from a deep pool of nothingness. Slowly, she opened her eyes. But their room was still dark.

"What time is it?" she asked.

"I don't know, but I can hear Mother and Father moving about in their room already. So it must be high time for us to get up."

On the other side of the bed they shared, Jane now began to stir as well. Hannah gave her a quick nudge to make sure the girl didn't fall asleep again, and then turned back to Nettie.

"You're usually the first to wake up. Are you feeling poorly?"

Nettie shook her head. "No, but I hardly slept a wink. I was wide awake for most of the night."

She tossed their blanket aside and got out of bed. The floor beneath her bare feet was uninvitingly cold and hard.

"Was it because of William and what happened at the market yesterday?" Hannah slid over to the side of the bed and got up too.

Nettie merely nodded. She had been worrying about him, the memory of Charlie and his friends going after him playing again and again in her mind.

"William?" Jane asked. She was sitting up in bed and stretched her arms while she let out a big yawn. "What did I miss?"

Nettie didn't reply and started putting on her dress instead. So Hannah answered for her, but she kept her voice low to stop their parents from hearing, since the so-called wall between their rooms wasn't much more than a few boards of cheap scrap wood.

"He was at the market yesterday."

"I know that," Jane said. "I was there when he and his father showed up and our father started a scene, remember?"

"No, silly. This was later in the day. When you and Mother were running deliveries and Father was off drinking."

"He came back?"

"Keep your voice down," Hannah hushed.

"And get dressed," Nettie added. "Both of you. Or we really will be late."

"Why did William come back to the market?" Jane whispered quietly.

Nettie poured water from a jug into their wash bowl. "He just wanted to chat. And apologise for that incident with his father." She scooped up some of the chilly water with her hands and splashed it in her face.

"That's very decent of him, I suppose."

"Yes," Hannah cut in, "but then a couple of our lads spotted him and they were spoiling for a fight."

"Why?"

"I don't know," Nettie said. "They seemed convinced William was involved in that street brawl two days ago."

"But he was with us that night."

"Hush, Jane!" She listened to the noises on the other side of the wall. But all she could hear was the voice of their father, so she safely figured he was probably too busy talking to their mother to hear what his daughters were saying.

"Sorry," Jane said, more quietly again. "So why were you so worried about him that you slept badly?"

"Because," Hannah whispered, "those boys then ended up chasing him."

"Oh no! Did he get away?"

"No idea," Nettie said. "We didn't see. And now will you two please get washed?"

"Girls," their mother shouted. "You're late."

"See? Hurry up."

Moments later, they joined their parents who were waiting to leave the house.

"Finally," Mother sighed. "I swear, the older you girls get, the slower you seem to become in the mornings. The market won't wait for us, you know?"

"Oh, Harriet," their father said cheerfully. "Don't be so harsh on our lovely daughters. They're young and they haven't got our decades of experience yet."

Hannah and Nettie exchanged a puzzled look. It wasn't like Father to be chirpy this early in the day. He was usually more the grumpy type in the morning.

"Come," he smiled. "Let us all go outside and be on our merry way while we enjoy the start of another glorious day."

Stepping into the street, Nettie wondered if perhaps he was still under the influence of last night's drink. And her mother had similar thoughts apparently.

"You sound very happy today, Henry. Were you lucky at the cards yesterday evening perhaps?"

"Nothing of the sort, my darling sweetheart. But I happen to have heard an excellent piece of news that made my heart sing."

He waited for his daughters to take the handles of the empty cart they had parked outside, and then the family started to trudge through the street.

"What's this news of yours then?" Mother asked.

"Yesterday, some of our lads got hold of one of those filthy ragmen. Taught him a proper lesson, they did." He was gleaming with pride as if he had been personally involved in the teaching of said lesson.

Nettie pricked up her ears. She was convinced he was talking about William running into Charlie and his friends.

"That makes you happy, does it?" Mother asked, rolling her eyes.

"I won't hide it pleases me that at least one of those scoundrels got what they deserve."

His wife chuckled. "Still angry about Father Michael pulling you and that Kirby fellow apart, are you?"

"The priest did what he felt was right. But luckily for our side, he wasn't around when the lads cornered that rat."

"Our side? Henry, you almost make it sound as if there's a war going on."

"In a sense there is, I suppose. Did you know the knave was simply strolling around at the market? Our market! I'm telling you these people have no shame. No shame whatsoever. But the boys showed him who's boss."

"What did they do, Father?" Nettie asked, trying her best to sound merely casually interested.

"The coward tried to run away, but they managed to catch him and gave him a good thrashing," he replied proudly. "Repaid him tenfold for everything he and his kind did to poor cousin David. They beat and kicked him until he stopped moving, and then left him in a pool of his own spit and blood." He laughed. "Who knows, the blasted fool might still be lying there, dead as a doornail. Wouldn't that be marvellous?"

"Henry, that's a terrible thing to say!"

"Nonsense, Harriet. This is a ragman we're talking about. They're more beast than man."

"They're human beings just like the rest of us, created in the Lord's image."

"You spend too much time listening to that priest if you ask me."

Nettie stopped paying attention as her parents slipped into the sort of bickering routine she had heard many times before. The only thing on her mind was William. There was a chance her father had been talking about somebody else. But she realised it was only a slim chance.

Pulling the cart beside her, Hannah shot her a worried look. "You don't think–"

Her sister didn't finish her sentence, but she didn't need to. It was clear they shared the same concern.

They slowed down, so there was a bit more distance between themselves and their squabbling parents.

"It has to be him," Nettie whispered.

"You don't know that for sure though," Jane said hopefully.

"No, but it's very likely, isn't it? I mean, William was being chased by a small group of them. It didn't look good."

"Maybe he got away. And maybe they ran into another ragman later and decided to beat him instead."

"Perhaps."

"Or maybe they didn't rough anyone up and they simply invented the whole story so they could boast about it in the pub."

Nettie appreciated her younger sister's attempts to keep their hopes up. But she wasn't convinced.

"You'll see," Jane insisted. "Tomorrow or the day after, William is going to come strutting up to you at the market, fit as a fiddle and with not a single scratch on him."

"Let's hope you're right," Nettie sighed.

But the image of William's body lying in a pool of dark blood kept haunting her.

Chapter Sixteen

Jane's prediction didn't come to pass. Days went by without so much as a glimpse or trace of William. Nettie grew increasingly worried. At night, she lay awake fretting over what might have happened to him. And during the day, her eyes were prone to drifting off into a faraway distance while her mind was filled with dark and unsettling thoughts.

Her work suffered too, but her sisters tried to make up for it and they succeeded in hiding Nettie's anguish from their parents. Mother probably thought her eldest was having one of those funny moods that afflicted girls and young women of that age. And Father was too busy being self-important to even notice his daughter's behaviour.

After a week, the fears and worries began to turn into a hollow sensation of sadness. Nettie wondered if she would ever see William again. Maybe the story had been true. Maybe they had beat him to death.

When a tear came to her eye, she quickly wiped it away as she didn't want anyone to see her grief. She and Hannah were manning their market stall and it wouldn't do for her to stand there crying.

But more tears followed, and no matter how she admonished herself for being silly, she didn't seem able to hold them back. And so she turned her head, looking away from their stall.

That's when she saw him. At first, she didn't want to believe her own eyes. Tears were blurring her vision, so she thought she hadn't seen right. But when she blinked her tears away and took another look, there was no denying what her eyes told her. It really was William!

The sight of him made her forget her worries, and her heart was flooded with an overwhelming sense of relief.

"Hello, Nettie," he smiled. "Been a while, hasn't it?"

"I'm so happy to see you," she sighed.

"As am I." His smile vanished when he saw the traces of tears on her face. "Have you been crying?"

"I was worried about you. I thought you were dead when I heard Charlie and his friends had caught you."

Only then did she notice the bruises in his face. They were clearly healing, but they were still various shades of green and black.

"Oh, William! They hurt you."

He shrugged. "They tried. I gave as good as I got though. There were five of them, so they had the advantage over me. But I managed to slip away from them in the end. Which is a good thing, because I'm sure they would have done a lot worse if I'd have given them the chance."

"I'm so sorry they did that to you."

"Not your fault. And I'm still here, aren't I?"

Fearful, she quickly scanned their surroundings. "Why did you come back? It's dangerous for you here. Someone might recognise you again."

"I wanted to see you."

"William..." She hesitated. She didn't want to ruin the moment, but she felt compelled to ask the question nonetheless. "This may sound rude, but I simply must know. Were you involved in that street fight?"

She gazed deep into his eyes, certain that she would be able to see what lay there – whether that be the truth, or a lie.

Bravely and openly, he met her gaze. "I won't lie to you, Nettie. Yes, I was involved in that fight."

She was sad and relieved at the same time. Disappointed to hear Charlie had been right to accuse him. But happy that at least he had been honest with her now.

He must have noticed her mixed feelings as well.

"I know you probably think I'm a horrible person. And you have every right to tell me to clear off. You only need to say the word and I will disappear and never bother you again."

Before she knew how to answer that one, he went on. "But first, I need to tell you something else as well. You see, I didn't want to be in that fight. We had arranged to have a few beers with some of my cousins. But Robert, well, he's a real troublemaker and he had other plans."

Nettie listened. She wanted to give him a fair chance to redeem himself. So far however, she wasn't convinced yet.

"When that fight broke out, the only thing I cared about was getting my brothers to safety. But by the time I managed to get to them, Robert had already knocked that poor lad senseless. I understand he was your father's nephew?"

Nettie nodded. "David's a cousin of mine."

"And my cousin nearly killed him. That's quite a complicated mess we have between us then. Is he feeling any better?"

"David you mean? Last thing I heard he was just fine again. I don't see that side of the family very often. My aunts are the disagreeable types."

"Family can be a handful, can't they?"

"Quite."

The inevitable silence that fell between them was painful and awkward. She just didn't know what to think of it all anymore. His confession had changed things. It had changed who she thought he was. She'd had such high hopes that he would be different from the other young men she knew. Him getting into a drunken street brawl didn't fit that picture however.

On the other hand, she told herself, when she asked him about it, he had answered her question honestly and without any hesitation or deceit. Surely, that meant something as well? But what?

Oh, what was she to do?

"Excuse me, sir," a woman popping up next to William asked. "What kind of potatoes have you got?"

"Only the very best, madam," he replied with the friendliest smile. The woman seemed to be under the impression that he was the one running the stall, so he decided to play the part.

He picked up a potato and held it up to her. "Look what a fine specimen of the humble spud this is, my fair lady. See its ample size. Feel its weight." He handed the potato to her and continued his sales pitch.

"It's a good potato," the woman agreed.

"That's because it's not just any old spud, madam! Farmers handpick these from the best English soil for us. Just imagine how pleased your husband will be tonight when you serve him a steaming plate of these beauties."

"My Ebenezer does love his potatoes," the woman grinned.

"But I'm willing to bet he will love you even more for buying him the best you could find." William winked at her and she blushed as she pictured the supper scene.

"You cheeky charmer," she giggled. "I'll have half a dozen, please."

"I shall select only the finest for you, madam."

Suppressing the urge to laugh, Nettie took care of the payment with the customer while William picked out six potatoes.

"You handled that extremely well," Nettie chuckled when the woman had left. "It looks like you might have a talent for the trade."

"Then perhaps I should ask your father if he would like to hire me," he joked.

They laughed, grateful the awkwardness that had troubled them earlier had passed so swiftly.

"A lovely thought," she said – *because it would mean I'd get to be around you every day* – "but I'm not sure it would be such a great idea. Our families don't exactly like each other."

"Really? I hadn't noticed."

They both giggled and she felt delighted to be sharing this preciously short moment with him, wishing it to be longer.

He interrupted the brief silence and gently took her hand. "Nettie, I would like to see you again. But you're right, it's a bit dangerous for me to come to the market. And it's not the best place to talk freely either."

"There's another dance in three days' time. Why don't you meet me there?"

His face lit up. "Do you mean that?"

She nodded. "Same place where we met the first time. After the market has closed."

"Great!"

They stood and smiled at each other, until he remembered they were still holding hands. He let go and cleared his throat. "I suppose I'd better leave now."

"See you at the dance. Don't be late."

"I won't."

Gifting her one of his wonderful smiles one last time, he turned and walked away while she watched him.

Behind her, Hannah cleared her throat. "So I take it Jane and I will need to go to the dance again this weekend, so you can be our chaperone?" she asked playfully innocent.

"If you don't mind awfully?"

"The things I do for love," Hannah sighed, rolling her eyes melodramatically.

Chapter Seventeen

William was whistling a happy ditty to himself as he walked home. He was pleased his chat with Nettie had gone so well. All week, he had been worried that she wouldn't want anything to do with him anymore. But she seemed to be willing to give him a second chance. What a relief that had been.

He would hate to lose a girl like her over something as stupid as a drunken street brawl that he hadn't wanted to be any part of. Because Nettie was different. He couldn't explain it, but he could feel it in his gut. And so far, every conversation he'd had with her only served to reinforce that feeling.

Going to the dance together had been her idea. It had been on his mind as a possible option of course, but he was glad that she had suggested it first. Because surely, that showed she was interested in him, didn't it?

He laughed when he caught himself asking that question. Usually, he was so confident and sure of himself. But Nettie was changing that. In a good way.

Again, he had to laugh at his own thoughts and feelings. It was all so delightfully fresh and confusing to him.

"My my," his mother said when he walked into the kitchen. "You seem very chipper this evening."

"Life is good and the world is a beautiful place," he smiled as he gave her a kiss on the cheek.

"Oh dear. What's her name?"

"Pardon?"

"The girl you're so clearly in love with. What's she called?"

William laughed somewhat sheepishly. "What makes you think I'm in love?"

His mother rolled her eyes. "Because men are about as subtle as a brick in these matters. Never mind. I'm sure you'll tell me when you're ready. In the meantime, be a love and go fetch your father for me. Supper's nearly ready and he's still at the pub."

"Probably drunk then."

"More than likely."

He sniffed at the stew that stood bubbling gently on the fire and took the large wooden spoon to help himself to a little taste. "Smells delicious."

His mother snatched the spoon out of his hand before he got a chance to taste the stew. "Of course it is, you hungry wolf. Now go get your father first."

"Only if you promise to keep Joseph and Thomas away from that stew until I get back," he chuckled.

"I'll see what I can do, but you'd better hurry."

"On my way," he said as he headed out the door.

Running to the pub, he thought about something his mother had said – *I'm sure you'll tell me when you're ready.*

Yes, he would have to tell his parents about Nettie at some point. It wouldn't be easy and he dreaded the moment already. His mother might understand, but his father was bound to disapprove. And that was putting it mildly. His father would be furious.

Perhaps if I presented it like a win, he mused. Make it sound as if Nettie was coming over to their side. That might please his father.

But then he shook his head and discarded the idea. More lies and deceit wasn't the way. And Nettie didn't strike him as the kind of girl who would want to play along with games like that.

He sighed as he entered The Black Swan. They would just have to take things slowly and wait for the right moment.

"There's my lad," Mr Kirby shouted when he saw his son come in. It was obvious that he was very drunk.

"Supper's ready," William said. "Time to come home."

"In a minute, son. In a minute. Come say hello to the boys first." He beckoned him over with one hand while holding a beer in his other hand. Even a simple gesture like that was enough to make him wobble on his feet. William knew the walk home would be slow and difficult.

Joining the group, he saw his cousin Robert was present as well.

"That pretty face of yours appears to be healing nicely," Robert smirked.

William's father threw an arm around his son. "And a good thing too. If those dirty market rats had killed my boy, I would have personally gone and squeezed their throats with my bare hands."

"Steady, Pa. Nobody got killed."

"Bloody shame they managed to grab you though," Robert said. William shrugged off the silent mockery.

"Aye," his father nodded. "Those scoundrels still have to pay for what they did."

"If you like, Uncle, the lads and I can seek out a couple of them and bash their heads in," Robert suggested helpfully. "William is welcome to join us... if he feels up to the task."

William wanted to wipe that sneering smile off his cousin's face.

"No, bashing their heads in won't do this time," his father grumbled. "We need something different. Something with more impact. We have to hit them where it hurts."

"Bashing their heads in will hurt," Robert said.

"No. Think, lad."

That might be a bit much to ask of Robert, William sniggered silently.

"Think what those market rats care about."

"Fruit and vegetables?"

"Money! That's all they care about. And that's where we're going to hurt them."

"I like the sound of that," Robert said. "How?"

"Do you know that fat oaf? The one who likes to pretend he's in charge?"

"You mean Mr Morris?" William asked.

"Aye, Morris. That's the one. He's bought himself a collection of shiny new pots and pans to sell. I say we steal them."

William's father paused and straightened his back, proud of the brilliance of his plan.

"And to make it even better, we're going to do it in broad daylight. Right underneath his big fat nose."

"Simple yet evil," Robert grinned. "I like it, Uncle."

"Well, I don't," William said.

"Why the devil not?" his father asked.

"Because we're not thieves. Street brawls and bashing people's faces in are one thing. But this is theft you're talking about."

"So what? They're only market rats. Stealing from them is like..." He waved his hand in the air, failing to find the right words.

"Stealing from them is nothing, is what your father is trying to say," Robert said. "What are you worried about, William?"

"Yeah, son. I thought you'd be pleased. We're doing this for you after all."

"Maybe he's afraid."

"Shut up, Robert," William shot back.

"Is that it, son? Are you afraid? Please don't tell me I raised a coward."

"No, that's not it! I just don't think that stealing from Mr Morris is the right thing to do."

"He's afraid," Robert said.

"I swear," William hissed through gritted teeth, "if you don't shut that big mouth of yours–"

"Then what? You're going to smack me, cousin William? I'd like to see you try."

"Lads," Mr Kirby growled. "You both need to shut your mouths. Robert, no more talk about my son being afraid."

"Sorry, Uncle."

"And William, we're teaching that bloated pig a lesson whether you like it or not."

"But Father–"

"Enough! Or I really will have to start believing you're weak. In which case you might as well go and live with those spineless market worms. Is that what you want?"

It wouldn't be such a bad idea, William muttered in his head. But instead, he just stared at the grubby floor and kept his thoughts to himself.

"You disappoint me, son. You'll never be a man until you understand these things. Those cowardly rats shamed us by giving you a thrashing. So we need to humiliate them twice as hard."

"Whatever you say, Father," William sighed. He knew it would be useless to try and talk some sense into his father.

"That's more like it. Now run home to your mother if you want your supper. I'm staying here to work on that plan of mine."

Ignoring the mocking smile on his cousin's face, William decided to leave without his father. *More stew for the rest of us*, he shrugged.

Walking home, he was determined to stop his father's nasty plot. It wasn't right. And more importantly, it would ruin the friendship or whatever else it was that he and Nettie had going between themselves.

He had to warn her. Betraying his father was nothing compared to the prospect of losing Nettie.

Chapter Eighteen

William seemed a bit preoccupied to Nettie. They danced and they laughed just like they had done the first time. And in many ways, she felt they were enjoying themselves even more now. But she also had the impression there was something on his mind. Something he wanted to tell her. She mostly ignored it though, putting it down to nervousness from his side. Which she found rather adorable.

After all, he wouldn't be nervous if he didn't care for her, would he? And so she thought she had a fairly good idea of what sort of thing might be absorbing him. But when he still hadn't spoken up after two hours, she decided to tease it out of him.

"This is fun, isn't it?" she said when they sat down to catch their breaths.

"It sure is."

"So you're happy to be here with me then?"

"Of course I am. I'm delighted you wanted me to come. Why do you ask?"

"Oh, I don't know. You seem a bit... distracted sometimes."

"Perhaps." He stared in front of him and then he laughed. "I can't hide anything from you, can I?"

Nettie smiled. "Haven't you heard? A woman's intuition never fails her."

"You're right. There's something I've been meaning to tell you."

I knew it!

"So tell me."

"I have to warn you though. It's a bit delicate."

"These things always are, aren't they?"

"And I don't quite know how to say it, because I'm afraid it's going to sound strange."

"How about you just try?" she smiled at him. "One word at a time." Sitting close to him, she looked into his eyes, willing him to speak the words she was sure he wanted to say.

"Promise me you won't be mad at me?"

"Heavens above, William! You really know how to test a girl's patience, don't you? Just say what you have to say. Please?"

"All right, I will." He took a deep breath. "My father intends to steal your father's pots and pans."

She blinked. "What?" That wasn't what she was expecting to hear at all. And her brain struggled to switch tracks. "What are you talking about?"

"I told you it would sound crazy. My father is bent on getting his revenge for that beating I took. And he's had this preposterous idea of stealing the pots and pans your father sells at the market."

"But why?"

"As I said, to take revenge. He's got it in his head that your father is an important man within your community."

"My father would love the sound of that. But then why steal those stupid pots and pans?"

"My father is convinced taking them would hurt more than having another round of kicks and punches."

"I'm afraid to say your father is probably right. My father's pride and his purse are more dear to him than anyone's physical safety – including his own."

"I don't know the details, but apparently he wants to do it during the day, right in front of your father's eyes. So I'm guessing he'll want to strike at the market."

She shook her head disapprovingly. "Will these tiresome games never end?"

"I tried to talk him out of it, Nettie. But he wouldn't listen."

"Of course not. Our fathers are both equally stubborn and equally foolish."

He grinned bitterly. "That they most certainly are."

"Thank you for telling me by the way. I appreciate your honesty."

"I couldn't *not* tell you about something like this, could I? He may be my father, but I don't want his dirty tricks to affect you or your family."

"That's sweet of you to say," she smiled.

"So what will you do?"

"There's not much I can do, is there? I suppose I'll have to think of a way to warn my father... without actually telling him what I know."

"Sounds like quite the pickle my father has landed us in."

She nodded and then the two of them fell silent, while she racked her brain with this latest development. All their fun and laughter had gone up in smoke and vanished.

He sighed. "I'm sorry."

"What for?"

"For having ruined our evening like this."

"Don't be silly. It's not your fault."

"We were having such a great time, you and I. And that's why I was hesitating to tell you. Because I knew it would spoil the mood."

"For what it's worth, I'm very grateful that you told me. And as far as I'm concerned, it's not you who ruined the evening. Your father did that."

"Sorry," he said as he dropped his head, which instantly made her regret her words.

"That sounded much harsher than I intended," she smiled apologetically. "Look, both our fathers are to blame. They're the ones keeping this bitter rivalry going. You'd think they were waging a personal war between each other."

"Yeah, it's one big farce, isn't it?"

"More like what they call a blood feud."

"I hadn't thought of it like that yet, but that's exactly what this is, isn't it?"

"Absolutely. Mind you, my father has good form when it comes to holding a grudge and ruining people's lives." The painful memory of her brother was still very real to her, even though he had died many years ago. "Sometimes I wish I could get away from it all."

"I know what you mean. And I often feel the same way. Especially at times when my father comes home in a drunken rage. That's when I just want to pack up my things and leave."

"My brother did that once. It didn't end well."

"You have a brother? I didn't know."

"I *had* a brother. He died."

"Oh. I'm sorry."

"It happened a long time ago."

"How old was he when he left?"

"Much too young," she sighed. "He was too young and too unprepared."

William nodded. "Yes, preparation is important. It's why I'm saving up some money and waiting for the right moment."

"Sounds sensible."

"What about you, Nettie? What's your plan?"

"I haven't got much of a plan yet I'm afraid. Other than not wanting to live with my parents for the rest of my life. I guess I'm waiting for the right moment as well, just like you."

"And what does the right moment look like to you?"

She shrugged. "Don't know. I suppose I'll recognise it when I see it."

"And when it happens? Do you know what sort of life you'd want?"

"Not really. Wait, that's not true. A happy life, that's what I want. Away from all this family nonsense and these senseless, never-ending arguments."

"Sounds like you and I want the same thing," he smiled. "But why wait? What's stopping you from seeking that happy life now?"

"My family. I wouldn't want to leave my sisters behind."

"Yeah, I worry about my brothers too. The trouble is though... someday soon our siblings are going to spread their wings and fly from their nest."

"I suppose they will."

"And where will that leave us, the eldest who stayed behind?"

She laughed. "Are you saying I'll be an old spinster?"

"You're too pretty to ever become an old spinster," he blushed.

"And someone as charming as you won't be a bachelor for long, I'm sure," she giggled. "Seriously though, I don't feel ready yet to strike out on my own. I'd be all alone."

He swallowed and looked her in the eye. "We could do it together."

She frowned, not entirely sure what he meant. "Together?"

"Yes, you and I. We could escape from our families and their quarrels, and start a whole new life – somewhere our fathers wouldn't bother us anymore."

"Together?" she repeated with doubt in her voice. This evening was full of twists and surprises. She had hoped he was going to tell her that he loved her. But now here he was proposing... what exactly? A life together? Marriage?

"Nettie, I like you," he said. "And I feel you're the sort of woman I'd love to build a happy home with."

"I like you too, William. But so soon... We've only just met two weeks ago."

His shoulders slumped in disappointment and he turned his head away, too embarrassed to look at her. "You're right. I've been much too forward. Please forgive me. Forget I even mentioned it."

Too late for that, she thought.

The way he sat there, he looked like a sad and rejected puppy to her. She felt sorry for him.

"I'm not telling you no, William," she said softly.

He nodded. "It's too soon. I understand."

She took his hand. "But I really do like you."

He looked at her again and smiled. "I've handled this rather foolishly, haven't I?"

"Not foolish. A bit clumsy perhaps."

"It's just that when I truly want something, I can get so impatient and then I–"

"Hush," she whispered, placing a finger on his lips. "Let's just forget about this business for now and get back to enjoying ourselves. Shall we dance?"

He nodded eagerly and stood up, offering her his hand. As he led her to where the crowd were dancing, her head was spinning. But it wasn't because of the music.

Chapter Nineteen

The air felt chilly on her sweaty skin when she stepped out into the night together with William and her sisters. Initially she welcomed the cooling effect it had on her body as well as on her mind. But soon she grew cold and so she wrapped her long shawl around her neck and shoulders, and hugged it closer to her.

"I'll walk you girls home," William said. "I wouldn't want any drunkards to bother you."

"Thank you. That's very gentlemanly of you," she smiled as she slipped her hand into the crook of his arm. They started walking, neither of them in any particular hurry to get home. She glanced over her shoulders to check up on her two sisters, who were following them at a short but discreet distance. Hannah grinned and gestured for Nettie to keep her eyes on William instead.

At least I know I've got two people I can always rely on in this complicated mess, she thought gratefully.

"Thank you for another wonderful evening," William said. "I've had so much fun."

"So did I."

"Oh, good. I'm glad you feel that way as well."

"Despite your rather premature proposition, you mean?" She was only teasing him, and judging by the slight blush on his face, it worked.

"Yes, despite that."

She chuckled, secretly pleased that he had put his cards on the table this early in the game.

"Were you serious?" she asked. "About you and me running away and starting a new life?"

He looked at her while they kept walking. "Absolutely."

She nodded. *Good.*

"So this isn't something you ask every girl the second time you take her to a dance then, is it?"

"Heavens, no!" He seemed genuinely shocked at the idea and she couldn't help but laugh at his reaction.

"You're teasing me," he said, sounding relieved.

"Yes, I am. And you don't have anything to worry about, my dear William."

"Why's that?"

"Because I haven't told you no, have I?"

A big smile appeared. "That's right. You haven't."

"Exactly. So just hold on to that thought and maybe ask me again later. When we're a bit further in this–" She hesitated, searching for a word to describe their relationship. "In this friendship of ours."

"Friendship? Or... romance?" He stopped and turned towards her. Behind them, her sisters' footsteps came to a sudden halt as well.

"I love you, Nettie."

It sounded like sweet, heavenly music to her ears.

"I love you too, William."

They stared into each other's eyes, with a faint and happy smile on their lips, knowing that those simple words were the key to an entirely new world for them.

Looking at his kind and handsome face, hovering so tantalisingly close to hers, she wondered if perhaps he wanted to kiss her. And if he did, would she let him? What would it be like to feel the soft touch of his lips?

No, she thought, stopping herself. *You need to take it slowly, Nettie. This is no time to lose your head.*

"It's getting cold," she said. "We should go home."

"Yes, we should," he replied huskily and without breaking eye contact. There was an intensity in his gaze that made her swoon and almost caused her to give in to the temptation of kissing those sweet lips of his.

Instead, she turned away and let out a long and blissful sigh of contentment. They continued their walk home, in silence. But it was a good silence – the kind that felt like a warm and happy glow. There was simply no need for words, since their hearts were doing all the talking, briefly connected in perfect harmony.

"Our house is up ahead," she said after a while. "So we'll walk this last bit ourselves. It wouldn't do for anyone to see the two of us together." She grinned. "Not yet anyway."

"When can I see you again, Nettie?"

"How about we go to the dance next week?"

"Do you love dancing that much?" he chuckled.

"Not particularly, no," she smiled. "But I love seeing you."

He beamed and took her hands. "Until next week then. And if I manage to pry any more information out of my father about his deranged plan for revenge, I'll find a way to let you know."

Ah yes, she thought. The revenge plot. She still had to figure out how to warn her father about that one.

"Thank you, William. Until next week." Reluctantly, she let go of his hands. Not seeing him for a week would be hard enough. But saying goodbye also meant the real world would be waiting for her – with all its problems and worries.

"Good night, Nettie," he smiled before turning and walking off. "Good night, girls," he greeted her sisters when he passed them by.

"Good night," Jane and Hannah giggled as they dashed towards their big sister.

"You have to tell us everything," Hannah whispered excitedly. "How did it go?"

"Yes, and why didn't you kiss him, you silly?" Jane asked.

"Because you don't kiss a boy on your second night out," Hannah said.

"Depends on who he is," Jane shrugged. "And William definitely strikes me as the kissable type."

Ignoring her sisters' frivolous chatter, Nettie said, "How did it go? Let's see. His father is planning to snatch our pots and pans. Oh, and William has asked me to run away with him so we can start a new life together."

Her sisters were speechless, staring at her with eyes wide in shock. Hannah opened and closed her mouth a few times before she managed to produce any words. "W–what?"

"I know. It's mad. And now I have to find a way to tell Father."

Hannah gasped. "You mean you've agreed to William's proposal?!"

"What? No! I was talking about his father's plan to steal our pots and pans. I have to warn Father somehow."

"Forget about Father's stupid tinware! You said William wants to run away with you?"

"He does."

"As in, he wants to marry you?" Jane asked.

"He didn't mention marriage."

"Nettie!" Hannah almost shrieked. "You're not seriously going to live in sin, are you?"

"Keep your voice down. There's no need to wake up the entire neighbourhood, thank you very much. And no, I have absolutely no intention of living in sin with William or any other man for that matter. The only reason he didn't mention marriage is because we didn't go into the details."

"Why not?"

"Because I was too surprised myself, that's why. We've only just met."

"So you're not leaving us yet?" Jane asked apprehensively.

Nettie drew her youngest sister close to her and embraced the poor girl. "No, I won't be leaving you two any time soon. William did seem sincere about it though."

"So what are you going to do?" Hannah asked.

"Don't know. Wait and see how things develop, I suppose."

"And what about this pots and pans business?"

"That's his father's idea. Mr Kirby wants to steal them in revenge for what Charlie and his friends did to William."

"Sounds to me like Mr Kirby's ideas are about as ridiculous as Father's."

"You're not wrong there."

Hannah shook her head. "What a mess."

"My sentiments exactly."

Hannah looked at her with sad and sympathetic eyes. "Oh, Nettie." She wrapped her arms around her big sister, so that now the three of them were engaged in a confusing but comforting hug.

"Promise me you'll take me with you when you run away with William?" Jane begged with a pitiful voice.

"I already told you, sweetheart. I'm not leaving. Not until you two are old enough and have found your own husbands."

"But you'll be an old spinster by then."

Nettie laughed. "Thanks, Jane." She disentangled herself from her sisters so she could look at them. "Listen," she smiled reassuringly, "there's no need to worry about any of this now, all right? So let's just go to bed. Some rest will do us good."

"Yes," Jane nodded. "And hopefully, when we wake up, all of this will have been nothing but a bad dream."

"That'd be nice. But I don't think so, my love."

Although sometimes, she thought to herself, *I'd wish my whole life would turn out to be merely a bad dream. It seems it's slowly turning into a nightmare.*

Some parts of it anyway.

Chapter Twenty

For days, Nettie was on edge. Every hour at the market was spent in a state of fear, as she wondered when the moment would come that William's father would strike. She caught herself scanning the crowds for his face.

But when nothing had happened yet after three days, she began to suspect Mr Kirby might not be committing the robbery himself. He was much cleverer than that, she reasoned. He knew her father would recognise him straight away if he showed up at the market. And what's more, men like him usually preferred to let others do their dirty work for them.

This thought only served to make her even more anxious however. Because now almost anyone was a potential suspect in her eyes. That young boy over there for instance – was he really just running errands for his master? Or had William's father slipped a coin into the palm of the lad's hand while whispering a risky dare in his ear? And what about the man who seemed to be taking his time to decide which potatoes he wanted? Could he be one of Mr Kirby's henchmen? And why limit herself to male suspects, if a woman could just as easily be persuaded to steal?

Nettie became distrustful of everyone who lingered and stared at their stall, keeping a watchful eye on them until they left. With every day that passed, she was turning more and more into a nervous wreck.

She realised she wouldn't be able to keep this up forever. But she still hadn't worked out how to warn her father either. How could she possibly tell him his greatest rival was scheming to steal his pots and pans... without revealing her romantic connection with William?

She considered telling him she had heard rumours. But she quickly dismissed the idea. Her father was normally the first to hear about any gossip at the market, and people would surely tell him about something as important as that directly.

And who knows, perhaps Mr Kirby had changed his mind in the meantime. Or maybe William had managed to talk his father out of it.

Men often bragged and boasted about all the grand things they would do. Especially when they'd had a few beers. But most of those plans never came to anything. Talk was cheap.

Maybe it was the same with this pot stealing scheme. Maybe she was making herself nervous for no good reason at all.

Still though, she mused as she gazed at their cookware on display, *it probably wouldn't hurt to move some of it into a safer position, would it?*

Yes, that's what she would do. No need to alarm her father, or to raise any suspicions. Simply move the pots and pans more towards the back, behind the fruit and vegetables, so nobody would be able to grab them and run off.

But she hadn't even moved two pans when her puzzled father walked up to her and asked, "What on earth are you doing, girl?"

"Just rearranging a few things. Putting them out of harm's way."

"Putting them out of easy reach for our customers, you mean."

"People are always eyeing them and picking them up. So I thought I'd put them in a safer spot."

"But we want people to look at them! And when they pick them up, that only shows they're interested. You clearly haven't got a nose for sales if you don't understand that."

"Shouldn't we be a bit more cautious about items as precious as these? After all, you paid a lot of money for them, Father. And when they're so easy to grab, someone might try to steal them."

Her father snorted. "Steal them? What a ridiculous notion, Nettie. These pots and pans are hardly like a potato. No one will be slipping one into their pocket, you know."

"I'm not joking, Father. It's only a matter of time before someone will try."

"What makes you think that?"

She shrugged. "It's just a feeling, I guess."

"Ah, one of those, eh? A case of that good old female intuition."

"You could call it that."

"Female hysterics is what I call it," he laughed.

"I'm not being hysterical, Father."

But if you keep laughing at me, I might have a fit.

He took her hand and patted the back of it. "There there now, my dear. Stop worrying your pretty little head over nonsense like that. Nobody is coming to steal our pots and pans. Now put everything back where it was and get back to work. We have customers to serve."

Grudgingly, she did as she was asked while he turned his back on her and walked away. "And to think the good Lord has blessed me with *three* of them," he mumbled.

Well, at least I've tried, she told herself. If her father didn't want to heed her warning, then that was on him. And any resulting incidents would be his responsibility, and his alone. Besides, the whole pots and pans idea had been his to begin with. So it was his money that was at risk here, not hers.

All the same, she knew who would be paying the price when or if the robbery took place. She and her sisters would need to work twice as hard and the family would have to survive on stale bread and thin gruel for weeks, possibly months, until the financial loss had been recovered.

And what for? All because of their father's daft idea of selling cookware. She had told him right from the start it wouldn't work. But just because she was a woman, her opinion didn't matter.

Hysterical indeed.

Silently grumbling to herself about her father's follies and the unfairness of the world in general, she didn't notice the trio of street urchins who had come sneaking up to their cart. The three boys exchanged a quick glance with each other and then the tallest one gave a short nod.

That was the signal for the other two to spring into action.

Chapter Twenty-One

Quick and nimble like a pair of street foxes, the two boys tipped over several baskets, sending heaps of onions, potatoes and turnips falling and tumbling over the dirty cobbled street. People muttered angrily and Henry Morris shouted as he came rushing to the scene. In the confusion, the eager hands of all three of the boys shot out at the pots and pans. They grabbed what they could carry and ran off like the wind.

"Thieves," Nettie's father yelled. "Stop those thieves!"

But they were much too fast for anyone to stop them. Most onlookers didn't even try. The other market people were too busy and too concerned about the safety of their own goods to abandon their stalls. And the crowd simply stared after the young thieves as they dashed off and vanished.

"Come back, you worthless thugs," Henry Morris shouted, shaking his fist while he ran a few yards in the direction they had disappeared in. But he soon gave up when he realised they were already long gone.

His face still red with anger, he turned back. "How many did they get?"

Nettie did a quick assessment of the damage, while her sisters hurried to gather the vegetables that had fallen on the ground.

"Five, I think."

"Five?"

Nettie nodded silently. Her father's face was turning pale now.

"But that's– That's horrible. I still owe money for them. Nettie, how can I pay back the moneylender if I can't sell the goods anymore?"

She could hear the panic in his voice. She saw the terror in his eyes. And as he stood there, trembling with fear, she couldn't help but pity him. He had brought this upon himself, going into debt for an idea that was bound to fail from the start. But that didn't matter to her kind and compassionate heart. Faced with misery, sympathy was her natural reflex.

And so she laid a gentle hand on his shoulder to comfort him. "It's all right, Father. We'll find a way. It won't be easy and we'll have to make sacrifices. But we will pay the money back."

He sighed and shook his head.

"You warned me about this sort of thing. And foolish old me didn't want to listen to you, even though you seemed so convinced of the danger. Almost as if you knew it would happen."

She squeezed his shoulder. "No need to blame yourself over that, Father. There was no way you could know."

She saw him clenching his jaw as he stared into the distance.

"Did you?" he asked suddenly.

"Did I what?"

"Did you know? You seemed awfully certain."

"Father..."

"Is that why you wanted to move the pots and pans out of reach? Intuition, my foot! You knew, didn't you? How?"

"I merely felt–"

Her father exploded with rage and shouted, "Did you know this would happen?"

It would have been so easy to lie. She could simply tell him it had merely been a feeling. Female intuition, just like she said. Eventually, he would believe her. But she didn't want to tell him a lie. She wanted to tell him the truth.

"William told me."

"Who's William?"

She swallowed. "He's Mr Kirby's son."

"Kirby?! Why would that scoundrel's spawn tell you?"

"He wanted to warn me."

"Warn you? About this?" He pointed at their stall that her sisters were now rearranging as best as they could. "He knew about this?"

"It was his father's plan."

"What?!"

"It was his son who Charlie and his mates beat up a couple of weeks ago. Mr Kirby wanted revenge. So he came up with the idea of stealing our pots and pans."

"I should've known that crook was behind this." He clenched his fists. "I swear I'll make him pay for his crime." Then he paused and looked at her, frowning. "And his son told you this? Why would he betray his own father?"

"As I said, he wanted to warn me."

"But why? If he's the one who got that beating from Charlie, then surely he'd welcome a bit of revenge?"

She paused for a heartbeat and then decided to just blurt it out. "He told me because he cares for me."

"He cares for you?" her father said slowly and incredulously.

"He loves me, Father."

"Oh, I see. You poor, naive girl. Has he been whispering sweet words and promises in your ear? If you think it's love he's after, you're sadly mistaken. Stay well away from him, dear."

"No, Father. You don't understand. He really does love me. And I love him too."

Her father remained silent and his face was impossible to read, devoid of any visible sentiment. For the briefest of moments, she was hopeful he might just accept what he had heard. But then the dam of his emotions burst and his rage broke through in all its forcefulness.

"You vicious serpent!" He grabbed her arms and started shaking her while his face turned a deep crimson red. "Of all the possible insults, this is by far the most hurtful and the most despicable! Have I been such a bad father to you? Why do you spite me like this?"

"Spite you? Father, I didn't do this on purpose."

"Be silent, you shameless wench!"

"Please, stop. You're hurting my arm."

He let go of her. But his eyes were still shooting murderous glares at her. "How long have you been carrying on with that filthy dog?"

"We haven't been carrying on–"

He slapped her in the face. "How long?"

"We met a few weeks ago."

"Where?"

"At a dance."

"See! I told your mother I disapprove of those vulgar gatherings. Nothing good can come of them. And now I've been proven right. Dancing? Debauchery, more like!"

"We haven't done anything wrong, Father."

"Silence!" He slapped her across the face again. "When did you know he was one of those vile Kirby villains?"

She hesitated. She knew he wouldn't like her answer.

"When did you know?"

"I knew that first night. He told me himself."

"What?! You knew who he was and still you decided to carry on with him? That's as disgusting as it is shameful!"

"We're not carrying on! We–"

Again, he slapped her and this time she shrieked, more out of frustration than pain – although her face was beginning to sting where he had hit her.

"We haven't done anything wrong," she insisted angrily. "William and I are in love."

The back of his hand came down hard on one side of her face and then he hit the other side with his palm on the return.

"What do you know about love, you stupid girl? You're nothing but an ungrateful daughter who would bring great shame over this family. But I shall put a stop to this lewd and sordid affair. Right now!"

He grabbed her by the arm and started walking. She struggled, but he simply dragged her along.

"Where are you taking me?"

"We're going to find that crummy dog whose son would use you to defile our family name and reputation." He stopped and looked at her haughtily. "Kirby Junior may have pulled the wool over your ignorant eyes, but he's not fooling me. I'm going to give that two-faced liar and his nasty old man a piece of my mind. And a taste of my fist."

He jerked her arm and started pulling her along again.

"Hannah," she called back to her sister. "Go fetch Father Michael."

"By all means," her father grumbled. "Perhaps the blackfrock can lecture you on your sins and loose morals. After I'm done with those two Kirby scoundrels."

Chapter Twenty-Two

People stared at them as they marched past the market stalls while her father continued to rant and rage. Nettie hoped he would run out of steam and give up his search before they found William or Mr Kirby. He would still punish her of course, and things at home would be awkward for weeks or however long he decided to hold a grudge against her. But that was preferable to any confrontation with the Kirby men when he was in this agitated state.

If only Father Michael would show up.

She was convinced the priest would be able to say the right words and settle everyone down. Just like he always did.

"Father, please. Stop this foolishness."

"Foolishness? It's you who's been a fool, child! Not me."

"But we need to get back to our stall. We can't leave Hannah and Jane alone for long."

"They'll manage. You didn't think I was going to let something like this pass, did you? Those rats stole from us and I intend to get everything back."

"So are we going to tramp all over town looking for them? You'll never find them."

"We'll see about that. They often hang about in the streets just off the market. That's where we'll start."

"And what will you do if we find them?"

"I'll make that scoundrel give me back my pots and pans. And then I'll tell him how I feel about his son."

They rounded a corner and she bumped into her father when he suddenly stopped. "Well, speak of the devil himself," he grinned.

A bit further down the street stood Mr Kirby and William with their rag cart. The two men hadn't spotted them yet, but that was about to change as Nettie's father stomped over to them.

"Where are they?" her father shouted angrily.

"Eh? I don't know what you're on about," Mr Kirby replied calmly.

"The pots and pans you stole from me!"

"How would I know? I didn't steal them."

"No, you let three snot-nosed ragamuffins do the dirty work for you instead."

"You're mad, man. Why on earth would I do that?"

"To have your revenge. And don't you dare deny it." He pointed at William. "Your own son over there told my daughter everything."

Mr Kirby briefly glanced at William and then turned to Nettie's father again. "Why would my son talk to your daughter? He's got more sense than that. Better taste too."

"Then it seems you're an even bigger fool than I thought. Your son has been trying to seduce my daughter, by pouring sweet words in her ears and exploiting the kindness of her heart. Just so he could have his wicked way with her and defile her honour."

"What honour?" Mr Kirby mocked. "My son would never sink so low as to lay with a costermonger's daughter. I mean, look at her. I've seen mules and horses that were a thousand times prettier than your girl."

"Why, you foul-mouthed imp! Don't think I can't see what you're trying to do. You're attempting to distract me with your insults. The fact remains you're a thief."

"That's slander! I'm a businessman trying to make a living."

"You ordered those street thugs to steal my pots and pans!"

"Says who? You have no proof."

"Your son confessed everything to my daughter, remember? He betrayed you, his own father, to win a girl's trust. Ha, the lad must be just as devious as you."

"Is that what the silly cow told you? Probably to hide the fact she's lusting after my boy, instead of the other way around."

"Are you calling my daughter a liar?"

"Among many other things, yes."

"Then why don't you ask him yourself? Go ahead, ask your son if it's true. Let him speak the truth if he has even an ounce of decency in his veins."

"All right, I will. William, did you tell that coster girl this preposterous lie of me wanting to steal their stupid pots and pans?"

William took a deep breath. "Yes, I did. And don't say it's a lie, Father. You know it's not. You told plenty of other people about your plan."

"Why?!" Mr Kirby turned red with rage. "Why did you do it?"

"Because I love her." He looked at Nettie and then at her father. "That's the truth, Mr Morris. I wasn't seducing your daughter. I really do love her."

"Love?" Mr Kirby said furiously. "What kind of sick and twisted mind lives in that thick skull of yours? Why would you even consider going anywhere near a miserable wench like that?"

"Stop insulting my daughter," Nettie's father bristled. "She may have been foolish enough to fall for your son's wickedness, but I won't have you calling her names."

"Is that so? Well, let me tell you, I've got plenty more names for the likes of you and your ugly daughter."

"Do you now?" Nettie's father pulled up his sleeves and took a defiant step forward. "Like what?"

"How about–"

"Father, please," William pleaded. "There's no need for this. Mr Morris, I'm asking you as well. Can't you both just accept that Nettie and I love each other?"

While their fathers were arguing, he had moved over to Nettie. Standing next to her, he now placed a hand on her shoulder – as a display of their bond.

But the gesture angered Nettie's father. "Take your grubby hands off my daughter, you vile dog!" He lashed out to swat William's hand away from her shoulder.

"Don't you dare touch my son, you dirty coster," Mr Kirby growled as he tried to block Nettie's father.

"He started it," Henry Morris said, his nostrils flaring with anger. "And Lord knows where else he's been touching her."

"Father!" Nettie said vehemently, disgusted by what he was insinuating.

But her father ignored her and glared at William. "Get away from my girl, I said." Roughly, he shoved the young man in the chest.

"And I told you not to touch my son!" Mr Kirby flew at Nettie's father and the two of them got into a blurry fist fight, trying to hit and shove each other.

"Stop!" Nettie shrieked. "Will you both please stop this pathetic nonsense?"

William tried to separate the two men, but they were blinded by their fury and in the confusion he got someone's fist in his face.

"Cease this riotous brutality!" Father Michael shouted as he came running to the scene. "In the name of all that is holy, enough!"

Grabbing both men by their collar, he pulled them apart. For a man of God, he could be surprisingly forceful when he needed to. William held back his father, while the priest placed a restraining hand on Nettie's father's chest.

"What's all this then?" he demanded. "I see it's a good thing your daughter Hannah came to fetch me, Mr Morris."

Nettie's father pointed at Mr Kirby and William. "That scoundrel's son has seduced and defiled my daughter, Father Michael!"

"No, he hasn't!" Nettie said angrily.

"And he did it knowing full well who she was," her father continued, ignoring her. "Just to bring shame on my family."

"There is no shame!"

"She's the one who did the seducing, Father," Mr Kirby said. "She did it on purpose too, like a wicked Jezebel, to turn father and son against each other and destroy the loving family bond we have."

Nettie let out an irritated groan. "Will everyone please stop talking rubbish!"

Her father wasn't letting up however. "And that treacherous thief stole my pots and pans, Father!"

"I did not!"

"Liar! Your own son confessed as much to my daughter."

"And you expect us to believe the word of a harlot like her?"

"Call her a harlot or a wench one more time and I swear I'll–"

"Enough!" Father Michael shouted. "I have no idea what this dispute is all about, but I must insist that you all refrain from using that sort of language."

Both fathers opened their mouths to speak, but the priest raised his hand to stop them. "I shall hear no more arguing from any of you." He pointed a finger at Mr Kirby and then at Nettie's father, to ensure they kept their mouths shut.

"It's clear there's a strong disagreement between your families, and there has been for a long time, I believe. We shan't resolve your differences out here on the street. I want each of you to come and see me in my church – separately. So we can discuss this problem like civilised people."

He looked at everyone, including Nettie and William. Their fathers were staring at the ground, visibly resentful but unwilling to argue with the priest.

Nettie was grateful for the interruption and for Father Michael's offer, although she doubted they would be taking him up on it. Her father and Mr Kirby were too proud and too stubborn for that.

The priest let out a deep breath, satisfied that for the time being at least, he had halted any further hostilities.

"Mr Morris, Mr Kirby," he nodded at each man in turn. "I want you both to go back to running your business and to forget about this quarrel for now. It serves no one's interests to fight like this in public. And please know that I shall be keeping an eye on you."

Under his stern gaze, the two men turned into remorseful schoolboys who had been told off for the mischief they had caused.

"Let's go, Nettie," her father muttered as he turned around. "The market is waiting for us."

"Grab our cart, son," Mr Kirby said. "We'll go find another spot."

Nettie and William stared longingly at each other, their eyes bidding a sad and silent goodbye. Then they each followed their father. Before she rounded the corner, she looked back one more time. Would she be seeing William again? She was certain she wouldn't be allowed to go to any more dances. And the market was probably out of bounds for William. So how were they supposed to meet?

Chapter Twenty-Three

Standing by the window of their bedroom, Nettie stared at the small, gloomy courtyard below her. There wasn't much to see, especially since night had fallen, and so her mind kept drifting off to what had happened earlier. Again and again, she relived the events of the day. Could she have said or done something differently? Should she have lied to her father?

Had it been a mistake to tell him about her love for William? In hindsight, it didn't seem like the smartest decision. At the time though, it had felt like the right thing to do. And anyway, it was too late now. *What's done is done*, she sighed silently. Regrets wouldn't change anything.

"Ouch," Jane said behind her. "That hurt. Nettie, will you do my braids, please? Hannah's useless. She's going to pull all my hair out."

"It's not my fault you can't sit still for a minute," Hannah objected.

"How can I sit still if you keep pulling my hair like that?"

Her sisters were on the bed, with Hannah positioned behind Jane to comb and braid her hair. But as usual when it came to these matters, they weren't getting along.

"Hush, you two," Nettie said. "I've heard enough arguing for the day, thank you."

"Sorry," her siblings said apologetically.

"No, I'm sorry. I shouldn't be grumpy with you just because Father and Mr Kirby were at each other's throats again."

Smiling, she hopped onto the bed to join her sisters. She took over the hairbrush from Hannah and gently started brushing Jane's hair. Sitting this close together with them, the world almost felt right again.

Almost.

"This is nice," Jane said. "I wish all our evenings could be like this."

"Me too, sweetheart," Nettie replied.

"It's always Father who ruins things for us, isn't it?"

"He does seem to have a knack for complicating our lives."

"Sometimes I think we'd be better off without him."

"Jane! You shouldn't say that."

"It's not like he'll hear me," her youngest sister shrugged. "Because he's at the pub again. And Mother is next door helping Mrs Wilson. So we can say whatever we want."

"That still doesn't mean you should say things like that though."

"Why not? Haven't you ever had thoughts like that? Have you never wished for a better father? One who doesn't waste all our money? Someone who loves us and takes good care of us?"

Nettie couldn't deny she'd had similar thoughts. But she couldn't say that out loud. It would feel disrespectful.

A knock at the window startled all three of them. Their room was on the upper floor, so who could be knocking at the window? And at this late hour no less!

Nettie got up and went over to the window to have a look. She was confused and overjoyed at the same time to see the smiling face of William staring back at her through the thin window pane.

"What are you doing?" she asked after she had opened the window. "How did you get up here?"

"I climbed the drainpipe," he said, clinging on to the windowsill.

"But why?"

"I wanted to see you."

"You're mad. You could have fallen to your death."

"You're worth the risk."

"Charmer. You'd better come in, before you lose your grip and break your foolish neck."

"Thank you," he groaned as he pulled himself up and clambered through the window. "Oh, hello girls," he said when he saw Jane and Hannah sitting on the bed.

Nettie's sisters giggled, excited and nervous about his presence in their shared bedroom.

"Mother and Father aren't in," Nettie told him. "But if they found you here, I'm sure all hell would break loose. My father has forbidden me from seeing you."

"I won't stay long, I promise. But I simply had to see you. And I've brought you something."

He took the burlap sack he'd been carrying with him and opened it.

"Our pots and pans," Nettie exclaimed when he showed her the contents.

"The boys who stole them gave them to my father this afternoon. I don't think he'd decided yet what to do with them. He just left them on the table when he went off to the pub to celebrate. So I figured I'd bring them back to you."

"He'll be angry with you when he finds them missing."

William shrugged. "I'm used to him being angry with me. And besides, it can't get much worse than today. You should have heard him yelling at me afterwards. Imagine his son falling in love with the daughter of his worst enemy." He rolled his eyes. "Ridiculous."

"My father was none too pleased either. He said he'd kill you if he ever caught you near me again."

William raised an eyebrow. "Do you think he meant it?"

"Probably not. He often says things to make himself sound bigger and more important than he really is. Still, I wouldn't want to put it to the test. Not with those words."

She gazed at him, imagining how she would feel if her father did ever kill him. She would be devastated. It would be like losing the only sparkle of hope and joy she had experienced in her life since a long time.

He smiled. "Don't worry. I won't let him."

"Oh, William," she sighed. "What will we do?"

"My offer still stands, you know."

She looked at him with a frown on her face, not understanding what he meant.

"My offer for you and I to run away from it all," he explained. "We can leave this mess far behind us and start anew somewhere else."

Her sisters gasped and from the corner of her eyes, she could see Jane grabbing hold of Hannah.

"I'm not sure it would be that easy, William," she sighed.

"Of course it wouldn't. These things are never easy. But I've got some money set aside. It's not much, but it should be enough to pay the rent, buy food and stay warm for the first few months. Once we both find work, we'll be able to pay our own way."

"But Nettie," Jane started saying with a deeply worried voice, before Nettie cut her off gently with a raised hand.

"I just don't know, William. There are so many doubts and questions in my mind."

"Like what?"

Like what if you grow tired of me and you decide to abandon me, she thought. Then she'd be all on her own in an unfamiliar place, with no one to turn to.

"We've only just met," she said instead. "How can we make such an important decision so soon?"

"I know," he sighed. "The trouble is our fathers are forcing our hand, aren't they? They won't ever change, Nettie. They'll keep fighting and coming up with petty revenge plots. Can't you see that?"

"Yes, I do see that. But leaving our families behind and starting a new life together is a big step."

"Maybe not as big as you think. All we'd have to do to get started is find a place to live. We wouldn't need much. A small room will do at the start."

"Just like that?"

Did he really believe it was that simple?

"Just like that," he nodded confidently.

"William, I don't want to be your common-law wife."

"My what?"

"Isn't that what they call it when you live together without being properly married? I'd be your common-law wife."

"Then be my lawfully married wife instead," he laughed.

"Marriage isn't a joke, William." His carefree tone irritated her. How sincere could he be if this was a laughing matter to him?

"You're right. I'm sorry. I shouldn't have joked about something as important as that. Listen–" He took her hands in his and held her gaze. "I *am* serious. I want to start a new life with you. And I'd love for you to be my wife."

"Oh, William," she sighed.

How could he say that? It hadn't even been a month since their first night at the dance. But when she looked at him – hoping his face would speak the truth – she saw a fire in his eyes. A blaze of passion and conviction. Her heart wavered, but her mind fought back. She felt so terribly conflicted and she wanted him to hold her. In his arms, she was certain the confusing world would go away. If only for a little while.

The sound of the corridor door opening nearly made her jump.

"Girls, I'm home," their mother said.

Without a moment's hesitation, Nettie pushed William towards the window. There was no time for goodbyes. He had to get out before her mother came into their room!

"We're in here, Mother," Hannah said, trying to sound casual. "We're braiding our hair."

"That's nice, dear."

William was nearly out of the window, but they could hear their mother coming. He had just disappeared from view when she poked her head round the large old blanket that served as the door to their room.

Hannah was sitting behind Jane on the bed, brushing her sister's hair.

"You haven't got very far, I see," Mother said. "Been doing more chatting than braiding, I bet." She looked over at Nettie, who stood in front of the open window. "Nettie dearest? Why is that window open?"

"I wanted to let in some fresh air."

"Well, you're letting in a lot of cold air. So please close it." She turned to leave but then stopped, as if a thought struck her. "Nettie?" Her mother eyed her suspiciously.

"Yes, Mother?" She tried to sound as innocent as possible, but her skittish heart was thumping hard in her throat. She hoped William was nearly gone by now. And that her mother wouldn't notice the burlap sack on the floor. It would be hard to explain how the stolen pots and pans had ended up in their room.

"You girls haven't been smoking tobacco, have you?"

"Heavens, no!"

"Good. I wouldn't want my daughters to get involved with that filthy stuff. A woman smoking a pipe is such an unseemly sight."

"Don't worry, Mother," she giggled nervously. "We would never smoke."

"Or do anything else that was unseemly," Hannah added for good measure, which earned her a warning glare from her eldest sister. The last thing they needed was to raise any more suspicions with remarks like that.

"I'm glad to hear it. Finish Jane's hair, my dears. And don't go to bed too late."

They heard her fumbling about in their parents' bedroom and sighed with relief. It had been a close call, all three of them realised.

Nettie quickly turned around and peered through the window. The courtyard below was shrouded in darkness, but she could see someone standing there, looking up at her. He waved and blew her a kiss. She waved back at him and then he disappeared into the night.

My future husband, she grinned jokingly.

Her mind cautioned her William couldn't possibly be serious about his proposal. But her heart told a different story. Could he be her ticket to freedom, love and happiness?

Chapter Twenty-Four

"Found your pots and pans yet, Henry?" one of her father's friends joked. The men stood huddled together next to a food stall, each holding a cup of hot brew to fight off the morning cold.

"Perhaps you should look for them in one of those shops that sell fenced goods," suggested another with a wink. "Because I'd wager that's where they are. Unless they're lying on the bottom of the river."

The men laughed. Overhearing their conversation, Nettie shook her head. She never understood why anyone would want to poke fun at other people's misfortune. Maybe it was a survival thing, she thought. When you're miserable, any misery that isn't your own can be a source of mirth, she supposed.

"Very funny," her father grumbled. "You'll be happy to hear I happen to know who stole them."

"Of course you do," the first man chuckled. "Those three boys did it. We all saw them."

And none of you lifted a finger to stop them, Nettie thought.

"Those lads aren't important," her father said. "They're merely pawns in somebody else's dirty game."

"Ah, so it's a conspiracy then, is it?" The second man poked his neighbour in the ribs. Once more, her father was the entertainment of the morning and Nettie could tell they were mocking him. Why didn't he see that as well?

"That's exactly the word for it, my good man," Henry Morris declared with a straight face. "A conspiracy! A vicious plot to ruin my business. And do you know who's the evil mind behind it?"

"Pray tell, Henry."

"That lowlife Kirby, that's who!"

"It's always him, isn't it?"

"Precisely. And now he has even started to involve his son in his wicked plans."

"Preparing to pass the torch, is he?"

"In which way, Henry?" another man asked.

Her father lowered his voice and Nettie strained her ears to listen in. "Well, I don't like saying this and it's a bit shameful, to be honest. But I can trust you to keep this quiet, can't I?"

"Of course you can, Henry." The men grinned at each other.

"Kirby's son has been trying to seduce my eldest."

Great, Nettie grumbled. Now everyone would hear about it. He might as well have shouted it from the rooftops.

"Your Nettie?" one of the men gasped, feigning shock while trying to hide his amusement. "Who would've thought it?"

She blushed when several of them looked over at her. But the colour on her cheeks wasn't just due to feeling embarrassed. She was angry with her father for spreading that story. He made it sound as if there was a bad motive to the love between William and her.

"And what's he done to your girl?" the second man asked, a bit too eager for Nettie's taste. "He hasn't... you know. She isn't..." He left the words hanging in the air, but they all knew what he was referring to.

"Heavens, no," her father said. "Nothing of the sort."

"Are you sure?"

Nettie was slowly becoming livid. This was her they were talking about! It felt degrading to be the topic of such a lurid conversation. She had half a mind to walk over there and put an end to it. But she knew they might laugh at her female hysterics as her father liked to call it. And that would be even more humiliating.

"I know my daughter. She may be as foolish and naive as the next young woman, but she wouldn't do anything that stupid."

"If you say so, Henry," the man replied, giving the others a fat, sarcastic wink. "If you say so."

"What's that supposed to mean?"

"Nothing, dear Henry. Nothing at all. But I suppose the more important question is, what do you intend to do about it?"

"I'm going to give that Kirby character a firm piece of my mind, that's what!"

"Again, eh? You've given that man so many pieces of your mind, I'm surprised you have any mind left."

The small group of men erupted in derisive laughter – except Henry Morris obviously, who only became angrier. "What would you have me do instead then?", he grumbled darkly.

"That's not for me to say, Henry. But listen." The man threw an arm around her father's shoulder. "Kirby has stolen your pots and pans. And his son has tried to dishonour your daughter. So maybe it's time for something a bit stronger than words, eh?"

"Proper revenge, you mean?"

"Your words, not mine, Henry. I'm merely trying to show you what it looks like to us. And I'm telling you, as a friend, that this Kirby fellow will continue to provoke you and humiliate you unless you take action."

Several of the men muttered their consent while everyone drained their cup and returned to their own stall. As soon as the group had broken up, Nettie rushed over to her father.

"What was that all about?" she hissed. "Revenge, Father? Will this nonsense never end?"

"Stay out of it, Nettie. You have no right to speak on this matter."

"And why not? Let me guess. Because it's men's business?"

"There is that. But in case you'd forgotten, there's also the small matter of your sordid affair with the son of the culprit."

"Sordid? There's nothing sordid or wrong about my love for William!"

"I see you're still blinded by this so-called love you supposedly feel for that son of a–"

"And you're blinded by hate, Father. Your hatred is so big, you only see what you wish to see. A horse wearing blinkers the size of a house would be able to see more than you."

"That's quite enough, Nettie!"

"Have you spoken with Father Michael yet, like he asked you to?" She hoped the priest would talk some sense into him.

"No, I haven't," he replied without any hint of shame or remorse.

"Why not?"

"I happen to be a very busy man, that's why. I have better things to do than listen to a priest prattling on about forgiveness and turning the other cheek."

"Father Michael offered to mediate between you and Mr Kirby! So we might finally be able to end this useless conflict."

Why was he being so stubborn?

Her father shrugged. "What do priests know about how the world works? And doesn't their own bible say an eye for an eye?"

She looked at him suspiciously. "You don't want it to end, do you? Do you take some kind of pleasure from all these fights and arguments, Father? Is that it?"

"That's a preposterous thought, Nettie. I'm a man of peace, you know that. But the fact is we've been wronged, and we have a right to seek retribution."

She paused and then said, "But what if there was no more wrong?"

"What do you mean?" her father frowned.

"You want revenge for the pots and pans that were stolen, correct?"

"That's right. We know who did it and I intend to get my property back."

She swallowed, but her throat felt dry. "Then there's no more need for revenge. We already have them back."

"What?! How?"

"They were returned to us."

"By whom?"

"William brought them."

"William? William Kirby?"

She nodded meekly.

"When?"

"Last night. When you weren't home." She hoped he wouldn't ask for more details. Because she didn't think it would be a good idea to tell her father that William had been in her room.

"So he's been to see you again?!"

"Only to return our pots and pans, Father."

"Why didn't he return them to me then? I'm the rightful owner after all."

"You weren't in." Strictly speaking, that wasn't a lie. Although she knew that wasn't the reason why William had chosen to come and see her instead of her father.

"Puh! He's a coward as well as a scoundrel."

"He's neither! What he did was very brave and very noble of him."

"What did your mother say?"

Nettie lowered her eyes. She might as well tell the truth. "Mother doesn't know yet."

"You mean you let that treacherous rat into our house while you were alone?!" Her father sounded utterly scandalised. "Have you no shame? No shame at all?"

"Hannah and Jane were present."

"So now you're dragging your sisters into your depravity as well. This has to end, Nettie! If you don't end it, I will!"

Glaring at her, he adjusted his cap and walked away.

"I don't like the sound of that, Father. Where are you off to?"

"You'll see," he shouted over his shoulder. "I'm going to resolve this issue once and for all."

"Father, please don't do anything foolish," she pleaded desperately. She wanted to run after him, but she couldn't just leave their stall unattended.

Maybe he was just off to the pub, she hoped. After all, beer and big words usually were her father's idea of resolving things.

Chapter Twenty-Five

Nettie rushed to the church as soon as she had the chance. If her father didn't want to talk to Father Michael, then she would. Perhaps it was true what her father had said about priests not knowing much about the ways of the world. But at least Father Michael was kind and wise, and he always tried to bring about a degree of peace and fairness in the neighbourhood. Which was more than could be said of the likes of her father and Mr Kirby.

The door to the church was unlocked, so she opened it and slipped inside. It was by no means a grand affair, but Nettie liked the sense of calm that seemed to wrap itself around her like a comforting blanket. There was no sign of Father Michael, so she decided to sit down in one of the pews near the small altar and wait.

The only light in the church came from a few candles here and there, and from the sunlight that shone through the coloured glass windows. Looking around, she noticed she was all alone.

Under different circumstances, she might have felt apprehensive or uneasy. As the daughter of a costermonger, she was used to being surrounded by the constant noise and buzz of the market. In here though, the silence felt like a gift. She closed her eyes and smiled, without fully understanding why.

Maybe I should pray, she thought. Father Michael was probably busy tending his flock and he might not come back for hours. Saying a prayer wouldn't be the same as talking to the priest and getting his advice, but she supposed it was the next best thing. And so she folded her hands and lowered her head.

But then she frowned. She realised she didn't remember the words to the Lord's Prayer. It had been so long ago. She still knew a few bits and pieces. Something about 'kingdom come' and daily bread. And she thought there was a thing or two about forgiveness in there as well. But she wasn't sure about the correct order and there were some major gaps in her memory. If she tried to say the prayer and it came out all wrong, wouldn't that make matters worse? Would God then be displeased with her?

Something as simple as praying and I can't even do that right, she muttered to herself. *Shows how utterly useless I am.*

Frustrated, she tensed up her folded hands, making her knuckles turn white.

Or maybe this is proof I'm a sinner, if even God is preventing me from praying for a solution. It was stupid of me to come here. I'm not worthy and I don't belong in a peaceful place like this.

Bitter tears had come to her eyes and she wiped at them with her sleeve as she got up to leave. But then she stopped. Father Michael was standing by the altar and he was looking at her with the kindest smile on his friendly face.

"Oh, forgive me, Father. I didn't know you were here."

"I kept very quiet," he smiled. "I saw you sitting there when I came in just now and I didn't want to disturb you in your prayers. But you seem troubled, my dear child."

She sighed and let herself sink back onto the hard seat of the pew. "I wanted to pray, Father. But–" She lowered her head, too ashamed to look at him. "I can't remember the words."

"That's quite all right, dear. Shall we pray together?" He came over and gently sat down by her side. "It's easier than you think, you know."

"I'm sure it is for you, Father. You do it every day."

Father Michael chuckled softly. "I admit that helps. But really, praying can be as simple as talking to Jesus. Why, sometimes I come in here, I sit down and I talk to our Lord."

"About what?"

"Problems that might be weighing on my mind."

"You have problems too?"

"Of course I do," he laughed.

"Like what?"

"For instance, when I see people struggling and I don't have a clear or easy solution for them. That's when I turn to the Lord for answers."

"And does He ever talk back to you?"

"Not in the way you and I are talking to each other now. But He most certainly answers my prayers."

"How?"

"By putting thoughts and ideas in my mind. Or sometimes simply by making me feel loved. That's when I know I can safely place myself in His hands, and trust in a satisfactory outcome."

"But you're a priest. Why would God listen to someone like me?"

"Why wouldn't He listen to you, dear? We are all His children and He loves all of us in equal measure."

"Then why aren't we all equally happy? Why do some of us have to live in misery?" Realising she had spoken in anger, she immediately regretted her words. "I'm sorry, Father. I didn't mean—"

"No need to apologise, dear. I understand. And believe me, lots of people share your confusion."

She wasn't sure she would describe what she was feeling as confusion. But she nodded and continued listening. He had the sort of soft-spoken voice that made you want to listen to his every word.

"Let me ask you though," he said. "Why do people suffer? Is it because of an act of God? Or do we suffer as the result of acts of man?"

"If you put it like that, then yes, clearly the latter. But why does God allow that to happen? Why doesn't he put a stop to it?"

Father Michael smiled. "If He intervened directly, how would we ever learn to become a better person? Instead of solving our problems for us, the Lord has given us a great power."

"Which power would that be? The power of love?"

"The power of choice. At any point in our lives, we always have a choice. We can choose to treat others with love and respect. Or we can react in anger, bitterness and hate. That too is a choice we make. Even though it doesn't always feel like it."

"But what if we're faced with an impossible choice?"

She thought about the choice she was being asked to make. Follow William and leave her sisters behind, or stay loyal to her family and endure her father's erratic behaviour that was slowly ruining everyone's life? That sort of choice seemed downright cruel to her.

"Important choices are hard, that's true. But they're never impossible, Nettie."

She sighed, a deep frown creasing her forehead.

"Listen to your heart, my dear. It knows the truth."

"I'm not sure anymore what my heart wants, Father. There are so many doubts tumbling and turning around in my head. Almost as if several different voices are talking at the same time and I can't understand a thing any of them are saying."

"Tell you what. Let's just sit here in silence for a while. I'll do the praying, while you try to make sense of those voices. One of them will be the voice of your heart. Follow that one."

"But how can I tell that voice from all the others?"

"You'll know it when you hear it. You'll feel it. There's no mistaking the voice of divine love. Be patient."

She nodded, not quite convinced it would do her any good. Following Father Michael's example, she closed her eyes and folded her hands again. At first, she felt restless. Too many conflicting thoughts and emotions, all fighting for her attention.

Worried that Father Michael would sense her unease, she slowly opened one eye to take a peek at him. She'd half expected him to be fixing her with a stern gaze, but instead, he was a vision of calm and peacefulness. His eyes were closed and his lips were turned up slightly in a relaxed smile. There was an air of serenity about him and when Nettie closed her eyes once more, she too felt more quiet and at ease now.

She decided to stop listening to her own thoughts and to simply enjoy the stillness Father Michael was sharing with her.

And by the time she left the church, her heart had spoken. Walking back to the market, she knew what she wanted.

Chapter Twenty-Six

"Where have you been?" her mother asked, sounding half-concerned and half-irritated. "When I returned to the stall, your sisters were manning it on their own. And your father is nowhere to be seen, as usual."

"I went to speak to Father Michael," Nettie replied.

"About yesterday's mess, you mean? Did your father go with you?"

"Father said he didn't want to talk with Father Michael. So I went alone."

"Typical, isn't it?" Her mother rolled her eyes at her husband's foolish stubbornness. "But then why did you go? Your father's the one who needs a good talking to."

"I wanted some advice. And Father Michael seemed like the right person to ask."

"Advice? What about?"

Nettie hesitated. She couldn't tell her mother she had wanted to ask Father Michael what to do about her dilemma with William. Or could she?

"Well?" her mother insisted.

"It was about something that's been on my mind a lot lately." She knew her mother would never fall for a vague answer like that. But it was all she could think of.

"Something that's been on your mind a lot, eh? Would this involve a certain young man from a certain family who's taken your fancy?"

Nettie blushed for having been found out. But at the same time, she felt a sense of relief. Secrets of the heart were too heavy to carry around.

She nodded. "So you know?"

"Of course I know. You've been acting kind of strange for weeks now. Don't think I hadn't noticed. I suspected you'd met some lad. And then your father told me about what happened yesterday. Including your little guilty confession."

Nettie stared at her feet. The word confession made it sound so wrong. So sinful. Was that how her mother felt about this?

"I have to say, Nettie dear, of all the lads in London you had to go and fall for a Kirby, did you?"

She looked up and wanted to say she didn't do it on purpose or to taunt them. But she was surprised to see two twinkling eyes and a grinning smile.

"It goes to show love's blind, I guess," her mother teased.

"You're not angry with me then?" she asked, not yet quite willing to believe her luck.

"Why would I be? After all, I once fell in love with your father, didn't I? That should tell you how blind I was!"

They giggled and Nettie felt all the tension disappear from her body. She was relieved and immensely grateful that her mother was more understanding than she had dared to hope. A sudden surge of tears came to her eyes and there was nothing she could do to stop them.

"Oh, come here, dear," her mother soothed. She opened her arms and Nettie gladly threw herself into that warm embrace.

"I thought you'd disapprove. Because of William's family."

"This stupid rivalry is mostly your father's doing, dear. For as long as I can remember, he's got it into his thick skull that he doesn't like Mr

Kirby. I hardly know the family, so I wouldn't know what to think of those people."

"William tells me his father is just as stubborn and quarrelsome."

"That's men and their foolish pride for you, I guess."

Nettie let go and looked her mother in the eye. "William's different though. He's kind and he truly loves me. No matter what Father believes."

"I hope you're right, sweetheart. I'd hate to see you get hurt. He wouldn't be the first to speak of love and then break a girl's heart."

She wondered briefly if she should tell her mother about William's proposal. But she quickly decided it was too soon for that. First, she wanted to talk to William about the decision she had made while sitting in the church.

"I know, Mother," she said instead. "And I had my doubts too in the beginning. But every time I meet him, something inside of me tells me he's truthful and honest."

"As I said, I hope you're right. I know you're a clever girl, so please don't do anything foolish, all right?"

"I won't. I promise." She gave her mother a hug. "You cannot imagine how happy I am that you're taking it so well." She let go and sighed. "Unlike Father."

"If you're really serious about William, then your father won't have much choice but to accept the truth. Eventually."

"To be honest, I'm not sure he ever will."

"Of course he will. This is your father we're talking about – a boastful fool who likes to use big words to impress people. And he loves a bit of drama, that man does. Puts him at the centre of attention."

"I used to believe that as well. But don't you feel he's changed? This business with Mr Kirby lately seems to have made him harder and meaner."

"Perhaps, yes. With your father though, it's mostly just wind. You should never take anything he says too seriously."

"I don't know. This morning his words sounded more like a storm. He was very angry with me. And he talked about putting an end to it. That's when he left."

Nettie wrung her hands. Those words of his still haunted her. They had sounded so dark and ominous to her.

"I wouldn't worry too much about that, dear," her mother said reassuringly. "He's probably drinking himself into oblivion as we speak. And by the time he comes stumbling home to demand his supper, he'll have forgotten whatever he was angry about this morning. You'll see."

"If you say so." But Nettie wasn't convinced.

"Trust me, your father should be the least of your worries." Her mother gave a dismissive wave with her hand and then she smiled. "Now tell me, what are your plans with young William? When's your next meeting?"

"We haven't arranged anything yet. Yesterday's shock took us both by surprise. But there's something I want to talk to him about."

"Then go talk to him now."

"Really?"

Her mother nodded. "Before your father comes back."

"But I don't know where to find him. I don't even know where he lives."

"Head on over to the rag shops and ask around. Some of the owners there are bound to know the Kirbys."

Nettie beamed with renewed hope and delight. "That's a great idea. Thanks, Mother. You're a proper treasure." She placed a kiss on her mother's cheek.

"Oh, shoo already. There isn't a force in this world that would stop two young people in love. Just be careful you don't run into Mr Kirby, all right? You'd best stay out of his sight for a while, methinks."

"I will," she shouted as she hurried away with a dainty spring in her step. Maybe her mother was right, she thought. Maybe with a bit of time, her father and Mr Kirby would relent. And then there wouldn't be any need for her and William to elope. How wonderful that would be!

Could she really hope for an outcome like that?

Or was she foolish to believe in fairy tales? William wasn't a knight in shining armour after all. And she wasn't a princess caught in a tower.

They were common people and she wasn't sure if happy endings actually ever happened to the likes of them.

Chapter Twenty-Seven

She found them at the back of the second rag shop she went to. William, his two brothers and Mrs Kirby were unloading a pile of rags from their cart and carrying them into the shop's storeroom. Thankfully, there was no sign of Mr Kirby. Because Nettie's mother had been right: William's father probably wouldn't take kindly to her presence. She waited a few moments to make absolutely sure he wasn't around, and then she went over to them.

William's youngest brother Joseph was the first to spot her. "Hey, Will," he nudged his older brother. "Looks like you've got a special visitor."

William turned round and smiled when he saw her walking towards them. "Nettie! What a surprise."

"A good surprise, I hope?" she teased.

"You? Always."

Just then, William's mother came out of the rag shop. She stopped and raised an eyebrow.

"Is this her? The market girl you've been seeing so secretly?"

"Yes, this is Nettie, Mother."

She came over, intent on having a closer look.

"Pleased to meet you, Mrs Kirby," Nettie said with a polite smile. "I'm sorry for any trouble I might have caused."

"Trouble?" William's mother shrugged. "It doesn't bother me much that you and William have been seeing each other. Raising trouble and making a fuss is my husband's department."

"It's the same with my father, I'm afraid."

"Men, eh? I keep telling this one," –she wagged a finger at William– "that if he ever becomes like his father, I'll smack him so hard his head will be spinning for a whole week."

Nettie giggled. She liked his mother's frank and direct manner.

"So tell me, Nettie. Do you really love my son? Or are you merely after him for his money?"

"Mother!" William protested.

"It's an honest question," his mother replied calmly, probing Nettie with wise and kind eyes.

"I do love him, Mrs Kirby. And I don't care about his money."

"Good answer."

"Any more rude or blunt questions, Mother?" William laughed.

"Your mother wasn't being rude," Nettie said. "She's merely concerned for you. It's what mothers do."

"Your girl's a smart one, son. I like her already."

Nettie beamed. This was going better than she had imagined.

"But listen," Mrs Kirby continued. "If you two want to chat, you'd better take her somewhere else, William. Your father could be here any moment."

"There's a park a few streets further down," he said. "I won't be long."

"That's not what a girl wants to hear, son. Take her for a stroll and don't rush. Just make sure you're back in time for supper."

William kissed his mother on the cheek and offered Nettie his arm.

"It was lovely to meet you, Mrs Kirby," Nettie smiled as she took William's arm.

"Likewise, dear. Now go before the old bulldog shows up."

Nettie and William dashed off and only relaxed their pace once they saw the first trees of the park.

"That went rather well," she said. "Your mother seems like a sweet woman."

"She is. My father's the troublemaker of the family."

"I know I've said this before, but your father and mine are very alike. Perhaps the two of them should start a club for grumpy fathers." She laughed.

"I dread to think what their meetings would be like," he chuckled.

They walked on, enjoying the brief silence between them. Then she decided now would be as good a time as any to tell him about her decision. It was why she had come to see him in the first place.

"William, I've made up my mind."

"About what?"

"About your offer. About... you and I."

He merely nodded and didn't say anything, while he gazed straight ahead. Maybe he was worried she had bad news for him, she thought.

"I've decided two things actually," she said. "Firstly, that I love you, William."

He turned his head and smiled at her. He opened his mouth to speak, but she wasn't finished yet.

"I've also decided I don't want to abandon my sisters. I can't bear the thought of leaving them behind with a man like my father. My mother is a good woman and she tries her best, but Hannah and Jane need someone who can stand up to Father's moods and quirks."

"I understand."

"But do you really?"

"Yes, I do," he reassured her with a smile. "I know what it's like to be the eldest in the house. You feel responsible for your siblings. Especially with a bullying father. But tell me, Nettie, how does it affect us?"

"What do you mean?"

"How do you and I carry on? How can we continue to see each other if your father has forbidden you to come anywhere near me?"

She shrugged. "I suppose we'll need to be careful for a while and just see each other without our fathers knowing about it. Sooner or later, they'll have to accept that we both have the right to live our own lives."

"You clearly don't know my father," he snorted. "Even the most stubborn mule in the world would change its mind more easily than that man."

"I thought you understood, William," she said softly. She prayed he wasn't about to tell her he couldn't agree to her decision.

"I do understand. And believe me, I respect your decision. It's just that..." He sighed.

"What?" she urged him gently.

"I don't know how much longer I'll be able to put up with my father. He really is a brute and a tyrant, you know. One of these days, I'm going to be so fed up with him that I'll pack my things and go."

"And when you do? Where would that leave us?"

"You know you're welcome to join me."

She shook her head. "Not now. Not until my sisters are old enough."

"Then I'll wait for you." He smiled and added, "They do say all good things come to those who wait."

"Am I a good thing then?" she teased.

"No. You're the best."

"Well, you certainly have a way with words, William Kirby," she smiled. "You should consider becoming a costermonger instead of a ragman. Customers would love you."

"Oh, but I don't intend to be a ragman like my father for the rest of my life. I have plans."

"Plans? Tell me about them." As they continued their stroll around the park, she suddenly realised something. She was enjoying this tremendously. Just walking next to him, talking to him, while the sun shone on their faces – it was such a simple and insignificant thing, yet absolutely divine at the same time. And it was something she wanted to do more often. With him.

"Perhaps this will sound silly or foolish to you," he said. "But my dream is to have my own shop someday."

"That's not foolish at all. What kind of shop though? What would you sell?"

"I don't know yet, to be honest. I quite like the idea of buying old things, repairing them or fixing them up and then selling them on for a profit. But not old rags. Nicer things for a nicer public."

"People with more money, you mean?"

"Precisely. I just can't picture myself sifting through dustbins and scraping by on a pittance until I'm old and grey. I want to make money. Not just for myself, but to help others as well." He laughed. "You must think I'm a deluded idiot for having a dream like that."

"Not at all. I think it's a lovely dream. And I'm sure you'll make your dream come true."

"What about you, Nettie? Do you have any dreams? What's your plan?"

"For a woman, there aren't that many choices in life, I'm afraid. Maybe that's why I haven't given much thought to the future yet. It seems all we can do is find a husband and raise a family."

"Nothing wrong with that," he smiled, taking a sideways glance at her.

"Depends on the husband. When I look at my mother and most of her friends, I wonder what they ever saw in their husbands. There's no love in their marriages. Or maybe now I'm being foolish. Maybe love is something that only exists in fairy tales or those cheap novels."

He stopped and took her hands. "I don't think you're being foolish. Love is real."

They stared at each other. He was so close to her. If she inched just a little bit closer to him, he would likely do the same. And then their lips would meet.

Would she dare surrender herself to that embrace? She was burning to find out what it felt like to kiss him. But she knew those lips of his would lead her to waver in her resolve. And it was simply too early for that. They had to wait. The time wasn't right yet.

"Perhaps we should go back," she whispered. "Someone might become worried about us."

He nodded, but hesitated to let go of her hands.

Chapter Twenty-Eight

"What are you so cheerful about?" Hannah asked while they prepared supper for the family. "Did you manage to see you-know-who by any chance?" Their mother was outside hanging up the washing and their father still hadn't returned. But Hannah felt it safer not to mention any names.

"William, you mean?" Nettie said.

Hannah's eyes opened a bit wider and involuntarily shot towards the window, to see if their mother wasn't about to come in.

"Mother knows," Nettie reassured her. "She isn't like Father, you know."

"And thank heavens for that," their youngest sister Jane said. "I'd rather drown myself than be forced to live with two bullies. Living with one is hard enough."

"Jane, how many times have I told you? You mustn't say such things."

The girl shrugged. "Let's talk about nicer things then. Did you meet William?"

"I did."

Her two sisters giggled.

"And?" Hannah said, eager to hear all the details. "Tell us what happened."

"And more importantly, did you two finally kiss?" Jane asked.

"We talked," Nettie replied, taking a mischievous pleasure in teasing her sisters by drawing out the moment.

"Talking's a good start, I guess," Hannah said. "What did you talk about?"

"The future. Among other things."

"Oh, you know I hate it when you're being vague and evasive like this! Why won't you tell us what you two said?"

Nettie chuckled and decided to put her sisters out of their misery. "William told me about his plans. He'd like to have his own shop one day."

"I knew he was a good catch! Lucky you. I'm assuming there's a place for you in that future?"

"We didn't discuss that part of his plans."

"What?" Hannah rolled her eyes. "Nettie, do you want to end up as a spinster? You may be several years older than Jane, but she knows more about boys than you do."

"Well, that's no wonder, is it?" Nettie chuckled.

"Hey!" Jane shouted. "Boys just happen to like me, that's all. But you haven't answered *my* question yet. I take it all this talking meant you two didn't get round to kissing? Again?"

"I should hope not," their mother said as she suddenly entered the kitchen. "Seeing a young man your father disapproves of is complicated enough. So let's wait with the kissing for now, shall we?"

Nettie and her sisters blushed and quickly busied themselves with their cooking.

"Speaking of Father," Nettie said, "where is he? Supper is just about ready."

"Your father is probably where he usually hangs out when he's not at home and not working. At the pub."

"But when will he be home?" Nettie wasn't particularly looking forward to it. Not after her fight with him earlier that morning.

"Who knows," her mother shrugged. "Once he's run out of money, I guess. But we're not waiting for him anyway. The four of us can have supper when it's ready. Just leave some for your father."

Nettie glanced at the stew they had made and gave it a final stir. "In that case, supper's ready."

They ate in peace, with Jane and Hannah talking about how their day had been at the market. Not for the first time, Nettie thought how wonderfully normal and happy their lives were without the trouble and headaches her father caused all too frequently.

Just when they were nearly done having their supper, a loud singing voice sounded in the hallway.

"That'll be your father coming home, my dears," Mother announced rather needlessly.

"With a belly full of beer probably, judging by his singing," Jane said.

Their father pushed the door wide open and gave them a stupid grin. "I'm back, my lovelies. Did you miss me?"

"Sit down, Henry. We left you some supper." Mother gestured at Hannah to serve their father's food.

"Great," he said while letting his full weight sink down on his chair with a groan. "I'm very hungry."

"What have you been up to today, dear?" his wife asked sweetly. "Because I didn't see you at the market. You were gone by the time I got there."

"I had some important business to attend to," he replied with another one of his stupid grins. Nettie wondered if he was drunk or simply being mean. He reeked of beer and tobacco smoke, that much was for sure.

"Would this be the sort of business you conduct in a public house, dear?"

"If you must know, yes, I did have a few beers throughout my day. But only because I was very thirsty from covering great distances."

"Is that so? You've been out and about then, have you?"

"I most certainly have, my love," he said as he spooned some stew into his mouth. "I most certainly have."

Nettie gritted her teeth. He was referring to his threat of ending the situation. She was sure of it. He was being much too smug about his whereabouts. What had he done?

Her mother shared her intrigue apparently. "So where have you been to then, Henry? You seem awfully pleased about something. Or is that merely because of the ale you've been drinking?"

"You women are always so nosy, aren't you? You just can't help yourselves. But all right, I'll tell you. I went looking for someone. He was hard to find and I had to cover a lot of ground. So I stopped a few times to quench my thirst."

"I see. And who were you looking for?"

"George Kirby."

"Oh, Henry! You didn't get into trouble again, did you?"

"Aha, that's where you're wrong, my dear Harriet! I wanted to find him so I could *end* all our troubles."

"You went to make amends?" Her mother sounded just as amazed and incredulous as Nettie felt.

"Not exactly," Father replied, grinning as if he was the world's wittiest man. "I wanted to find Kirby, but I didn't want him to see me."

Mother narrowed her eyes in suspicion. "Why?"

"I wanted to follow him and see where he lives."

"That's a nasty thing to do, Henry Morris. And did you succeed?"

"I did, eventually."

"So you followed that poor man home. And then what did you do?"

"I waited." He wiped his mouth with his sleeve.

"You waited? For what?"

"I waited very patiently until I was sure they were all inside having their supper." He casually shoved his empty bowl away. "And then I set fire to their house."

"You did what?!" Nettie shrieked.

"Henry, you must be kidding! Please tell me this is some deranged and twisted jest of yours?"

"No, it's not. I set fire to a pile of rags at the back of their house. You should have seen the flames. It was a beautiful sight."

"Have you lost your mind?!" Nettie shouted at him.

"Mind your tongue," he shouted back, pointing a finger at her as a warning. "It was only a small fire. I'm sure they managed to put it out in the end. But at least they'll have understood the message."

"Henry, that's horrible. How could you do such a thing?"

"Someone could have got hurt, Father! And what if they weren't able to put the fire out? Maybe they're all dead!"

"Rats like them aren't that easy to kill, Nettie."

"They're not rats! They're people like you and me. William has a mother and two younger brothers, don't you know? They could be seriously hurt. Or lying dead underneath the burnt rubble of their house."

"If the little rats take after their father and they're dead, then I deserve a medal for services rendered to the good of society."

"You disgust me," she yelled. "You horrible man!" Unable to control herself, she flew at him, her arms and hands flailing wildly and trying to hit him where she could.

But he was bigger and stronger than her. He easily deflected her angry blows and then slapped her hard across the face.

The hot pain on her cheek and the metallic taste of blood in her mouth brought her back to her senses. "You're not my father," she growled, shooting him a hateful glare.

Not waiting for a reply and not wanting him to see the tears that were welling up, she fled from the room.

"Nettie, where are you going?" her mother asked worriedly. "Nettie, dear! Come back!"

But Nettie had no desire to turn back. She couldn't live under the same roof with a cowardly monster who set fire to innocent people's homes.

She simply couldn't. Not ever again. Not after this.

Chapter Twenty-Nine

Tears were rolling down her cheeks as she wandered aimlessly through the streets. Darkness was setting in rapidly and more than one roaming drunkard accosted her. But Nettie didn't care. She hardly even noticed them with their unwanted attentions and their leering stares. Her world had just been shattered. Perhaps William was unharmed. Or perhaps his body had been reduced to ashes by a fire that had engulfed his home. The truth was she simply didn't know. And that uncertainty drove her insane with grief and sadness.

But there was anger too. How could her father have done such a dreadful thing? He had hated Mr Kirby for as long as she could remember. Why? What had started it? She had no idea. And she doubted whether he still knew himself. Probably some petty disagreement many years ago – the kind of minor grievance puffed-up, self-important men like them would have a falling-out over.

Whatever it was, it had now led to this: arson. How utterly despicable! In her imagination, she saw horrible images of flames and she heard people crying out in panic as they feared for their lives. And knowing William, he wouldn't just have fled from the danger. No, if their house had caught fire, he would first have wanted to save his mother and his brothers – maybe even his father – with no regard for his own physical safety.

The sheer possibility he might have perished through this appalling act of her very own father made her feel sick. She started having trouble breathing and she had to stop walking. Leaning with one hand against a crumbling old wall, she placed her other hand on her chest. Her heart was thumping wildly and her stomach lurched with dread.

"You all right, love?" a man asked her with a drunken slur. "You look like you could do with a little drink." He stumbled up to her and bumped into the wall. "Here, try some of this," he said, holding up a bottle right in front of her face. "My best friend made it."

"No, thank you." She wrinkled her nose at the strong smell of alcohol that emanated from the man's bottle as well as his reeking mouth.

"Go on, love. You don't know what you're missing. This stuff will cheer you right up. It's never failed me."

"I said, no thank you."

She took a sideways step away from him. But he mirrored her move and grabbed her arm. "Doctor's orders," he joked.

Instead of being afraid, she suddenly felt very angry. Not just at him, but at all men like him. A flash of rage surged up from within her and she found herself giving the man a forceful shove that sent him stumbling back. He fell over and she heard the breaking of glass.

"My bottle," he wailed. "You broke my bottle!"

Nettie ran away before he had a chance to get back on his feet, although he seemed more distressed about the loss of his bottle than about her escaping from him.

The encounter had helped her in an odd way. Her head felt clearer now and she could think straight again.

I must find William, she told herself. Dead, injured or alive, she had to know. The only trouble was, she hadn't the slightest idea where he lived. Her father knew, but she could hardly go back home and ask him.

Looking around to get her bearings, she realised she hadn't strayed that far from home yet. So she decided to make her way to the rag shops. They'd be long closed by now, but perhaps there would still be people on the street who could direct her to where the ragmen lived. It was a small chance, but it was the only hope she had. Even though she dreaded to think what sort of people might be loafing about on the street at this time of day.

But what would she do if she couldn't find William tonight? She'd have to wait until morning when the shops opened and she could ask the shop owners. Did that mean she would need to find a place to sleep? She shivered at the thought of sleeping somewhere in an alley or under a bridge. Perhaps it would be better to stay awake all night in that case.

And what if she did locate William's house and she found out he was dead? Her stomach tightened into a hard knot when it dawned on her: without him, she had no plan for her future! Would she have to crawl back to her father? Never! She'd sooner die, she decided.

And without William, death seemed like the better option anyway.

"Nettie," someone called out her voice. She looked up and her heart jumped with delight when she saw a figure running towards her from the other end of the street.

"William," she shouted as she ran to meet him.

Throwing herself into his arms, she grabbed hold of him and squeezed hard to make sure it was really him. "Thank heavens you're alive," she sighed. "I was so worried about you. I thought you were dead. I thought I'd lost you."

"I'm fine, my love," he whispered while he stroked her hair.

When she pressed her face to his chest, the smell of smoke on his clothes was undeniable. "The fire," she said frantically as she looked up at him. "Did it hurt you? Is your family safe? Your mother? And your brothers?"

"Yes, we're all fine. How did you know there was a fire?"

"I..." She couldn't bring herself to tell him and burst out in tears instead.

"There was a lot of smoke when a pile of rags caught fire at the back of the house," he explained. "But luckily, my brothers and I managed to put out the flames before they did any real damage. My father is livid though. He thinks someone started the fire on purpose."

"I'm afraid he's right." She swallowed. She owed William the truth. "My father set fire to those rags."

She watched his face for his reaction, but his expression seemed to remain blank.

"I see," he merely said. "We all suspected as much."

"I'm so sorry, William! I swear I didn't know. I never even thought he'd be capable of doing something like that." She blurted out the words quickly and anxiously. "He came home this evening, arrogant and drunk. He sat down to have his supper and then he told us what he'd done. He seemed so proud of himself! I wanted to hit him."

"Calm down," he soothed, softly taking her by her forearms. "It's not your fault. Your father's the culprit here, not you." He wrapped his arms around her again and she surrendered to his warm embrace.

"What are you doing out here on the street anyway?" he asked. "You know it's not safe."

"I couldn't stay in the same house as that murderous beast! I had to leave. I had to see you. I wanted to know if you were safe. And I wanted to be with you. But I didn't know where you live."

"Hush, you've found me now," he smiled. "You're lucky I came to find you as well. My father's furious and he felt certain your father was behind it. There's no telling what he'll do next. So I wanted to come and warn you."

"I've had enough of this madness," she said tearfully. "You were right, William. I thought with time our fathers might change their minds. But I was wrong. They won't ever change. And this stupid fight will never stop. Until one day, someone's going to get seriously hurt."

"I'd say they came mighty close tonight."

"Precisely. And I'm fed up." With her head resting against his chest, she could hear his comforting heartbeat. She took a deep breath. "Does your offer still stand?"

Her eyes were open and she didn't dare look at him, but she thought his heart started beating a little faster.

"Yes," he said calmly.

"Then please take me away from all this. I can't go back home. I don't want to. You said you had a plan. So let's leave, you and I."

"All right." His voice sounded soft and tender. He lifted her chin up with his finger so they looked each other in the eye. "But first, there's something else we need to do."

Chapter Thirty

William smiled at her and took her hands in his. "Before we leave, and before we start a new life, I want to marry you. Nettie, will you be my wife?"

"Yes," she replied softly, swooning inside.

"Good. Let's do it now, straight away. Let's find Father Michael and ask him to marry us. So our future can start. Unless..." He seemed to consider something. "Unless you want to make it more formal? Or invite your sisters?"

She shook her head. There simply wasn't any time for a proper wedding with guests and a celebration. And no money either. "No, let's just get married. Father Michael will make it right."

Part of her would have loved to have her sisters present when she and William exchanged their vows. She could picture them as her bridesmaids, wearing pretty flowers in their hair. But then her father would know about it too and she was afraid he'd try to stop the wedding. She'd rather have an improvised secret wedding ceremony than risk him ruining the whole thing. That man had caused enough hurt and damage in his lifetime.

William gave her hands a little squeeze and beamed at her. "I love you, Nettie. This may not be the kind of wedding most girls dream of, but please don't worry. Our love will see us through everything."

She placed a soft kiss on his lips. "I love you too, William. And I don't care much about what sort of wedding we're having. As long as you and I are joined in love before God."

"We will be, my darling."

She nodded and tugged at his arm, willing herself to spring into action. "Let's go then. Let's find Father Michael and get married."

"He'll be surprised to see us," William chuckled as they started heading in the direction of the church. "I bet he's never married anyone in the middle of the night before."

"Do you think he'll agree to marry us like this? What if he refuses?"

"Why would he refuse to marry us?"

"I don't know. He might feel we're being too quick and too rash in our decision. And I'm sure he knows our fathers would never agree to our marriage."

"Father Michael doesn't strike me as that type of person. He's kind and he's got a heart of gold. He might think the hour is a bit unusual, but I can't see him turning away two people who love each other."

Soon after they had knocked at the door of the priest's home, William's prediction turned out to be right. On both counts.

The bleary-eyed priest blinked when he heard what they wanted from him, but then he quickly opened his door wide and invited them in.

"Come inside, my dear children. And please forgive my appearance." It was clear he had hastily thrown a long coat over his nightshift. "I usually retire early."

"We're sorry to have woken you, Father," Nettie said. "Would you like us to return tomorrow instead?"

"Nonsense, my dear. The Lord's work knows no hour and I'm sure you must have your reasons." He led them into his small parlour. "Please sit. I see the coals in the fireplace are still smouldering a bit. I'll stir up a fire again and make us some tea. And then you can tell me all about your story."

Once the fire was going and the priest had poured them a steaming hot cup of tea, they told him everything. They told him how they had met and fallen in love. They told him of the plans they had made, while their fathers continued their mindless vendetta against each other.

Father Michael listened and nodded. He gasped with shock when Nettie told him about what her father had done only a few hours earlier. He asked William several times if his family was safe and unharmed.

"I should have been firmer with your fathers," he admonished himself. "And I should have visited them myself. I had an inkling they wouldn't come to see me when I asked them to. How incredibly foolish of me not to have acted on that feeling. This tragic incident is partly my fault."

"That's not true, Father," Nettie said. "You did what you could. Just like you always do. The blame lies entirely with my father."

"And with mine too," William added.

"Perhaps," the priest said, shaking his head to dismiss the issue of guilt for the moment. He gazed in the direction of the window. The curtains were drawn obviously and the distracted expression on his face made Nettie suspect he was reflecting on everything he had just heard.

"And now the two of you would like me to marry you?" he mused. "So you can be husband and wife, and free yourselves from this dreadful ordeal?"

"Yes, please," she nodded. William gently placed his hand over hers and tried to give her a reassuring smile. But she could tell he was nervous too. She prayed the priest wouldn't say no.

Father Michael looked at each of them in turn with those wise and friendly eyes of his.

"Let's get ourselves down to the church then, shall we?" he said.

Overjoyed, Nettie wanted to jump up and hug someone. But instead, she and William clasped hands.

"Thank you, Father," he said.

"Thank you, Father Michael," she sighed with relief. "We were worried you might think our marriage was a bad idea."

"Most people take longer to reach that sort of decision. I'll grant you that," Father Michael grinned. "But as a priest, I've had plenty of young couples standing before me. And I know love when I see it, believe me. Yours is a rare and precious thing, and it will be my pleasure to tie the knot for you."

Nettie and William smiled at each other.

"And I must admit," the priest continued, "my hope is your marriage will finally force your fathers to reconcile."

He set down his cup of tea and stood up. "Now let's get started. We've got work to do. You may have decided to go ahead with this wedding on the spur of the moment, but I'll make sure you get a beautiful ceremony."

An hour later, the nave of the small church was bathing in the soft glow of candles and the sweet scent of incense. Nettie and William stood facing the priest close to the altar.

Since there were only the three of them, Father Michael spoke with a soft voice, almost like a whisper. And it made for an intimate and private atmosphere, even in the empty church. The priest said a few simple prayers that matched the spirit of their ceremony, and then it was time for Nettie and William to exchange their vows.

They looked deep into each other's eyes and faithfully repeated what Father Michael whispered to them, meaning every single word of it.

"I don't suppose you have a ring for your bride, do you?" Father Michael asked.

"As a matter of fact, I do," William replied.

To Nettie's surprise, he reached into his pocket and produced something that did indeed resemble a ring.

"It's not a proper wedding band," he grinned apologetically. "But it's the best I could do. I made it from a shiny button and a piece of string while Father Michael was lighting all the candles."

"It's the most beautiful ring I've ever seen," she smiled.

Carefully, he slid the ring on her finger.

"And it even fits," Father Michael chuckled. "What an ingenious young man you're marrying, dear Nettie."

He spread his arms to make it official and said, "Here, before the eyes of our Lord, I now pronounce you husband and wife."

Nettie's vision grew hazy as tears filled her eyes. But her lips had no trouble finding William's for their first ever kiss.

Chapter Thirty-One

Nettie woke up shortly after dawn. Golden rays of sunshine fell through the small window of the attic room. Father Michael had graciously allowed them to sleep there after their wedding. It was located in the old warehouse that served the priest and his nuns as a school, hospital, soup kitchen and whatever other use was required. She and William had been exhausted after the topsy-turvy events of the previous day. And when they finally lay down on the bed, they had fallen asleep in each other's arms almost instantly.

Now she opened up her eyes and smiled when she saw William lying next to her, still fast asleep. Not wishing to disturb him, she studied his face. He looked so peaceful in his sleep. So happy. She even thought she spotted a faint smile on his lips, but she thought that might have been her imagination.

My husband, she sighed blissfully. She could hardly believe it was real. But the ring on her finger told her their wedding had actually happened. She grinned. How quaint and utterly delightful of him to have made a ring for her from a few things tucked away in his pocket. Lying on her back on the straw mattress, she stretched out her arm in the air and admired her ring. It was only a button and a piece of string, but she would cherish it forever.

The straw in the mattress made a rustling noise when William stirred. She rolled over to her side so she lay facing him.

"Good morning," she whispered sweetly the moment he opened his sleepy eyes.

A smile more radiant than the sunrise appeared on his face. "Good morning. Please tell me last night wasn't a dream?"

"It wasn't," she giggled. "You and I are husband and wife."

"Good. Just wanted to make sure. Because otherwise, I'd do it all over again in a heartbeat."

When she kissed his lips, he took her in his strong arms and rolled her on top of him.

"So what do you want to do first today?" he asked. "Shall we enjoy our honeymoon in the attic for a little while longer?"

"A tempting proposition." She gave him another kiss, rolled back to her side of the mattress and sat up. "But there's something else I need to do first."

"Which is?"

"I want to see my sisters and tell them. I know that's not the most romantic thing, but please William? They'll be worried sick about me if I just disappear. As much as I love you with all my heart and soul, I'd feel terribly guilty frolicking around with you up here while they're left in the dark."

He smiled. "Don't worry, I understand. My brothers probably feel the same way about me. I'll go home to say goodbye to them. And I need to retrieve my money as well. I keep it underneath a floorboard in the bedroom."

"I have no money, I'm afraid," she said, lowering her head in shame. "Not much of a dowry, is it?"

"I don't want a dowry," he chuckled. "I've got you and that's all I need."

"We might need a roof over our heads though," she said before reaching over and planting a little kiss on the tip of his nose.

"Don't worry about that, my love. I've saved up enough money to pay the rent for a few months." He stood up and grabbed his clothes. "Let's go say goodbye to our families first and then we can start looking for a small room."

She nodded and tried to put on a brave face for him. It sounded so simple the way he put it. But she knew saying goodbye to her sisters would be the hardest part of all.

You want this, Nettie, she had to remind herself. A better future, away from Father and his insufferable behaviour. Real love, with a man who genuinely cared. That's what lay ahead of her now. She should have been the happiest woman in the world this morning. And yet...

"It's going to be all right," William said when he saw the worried frown on her face.

"I know."

But then why did she feel like crying?

She was nervous when she entered the market an hour later. *Please Lord, don't let my father be there*, she prayed. Telling her mother and sisters she was leaving would be painful enough. She didn't need her father causing one of his scenes.

And what if he does, a braver, more defiant inner voice asked? She was a grown woman, old enough to make her own decisions in life. He could either accept those choices... or rant and rage as much as he liked. His opinion wouldn't change a thing. She was a married woman now.

"Nettie!"

Jane had seen her first and she came running to her eldest sister. "Where were you? You were gone all night, and then when you still hadn't come back this morning, Hannah and I thought something awful must have happened to you."

They hugged.

"Everything's fine, my darling. Where's Father?"

"He's around here somewhere. Probably blathering someone's ears off. He said he didn't care that you hadn't come home. But I think he was lying. I think he was smouldering inside that you had run away."

Anxiously, Nettie's eyes turned left and right. But there was no sign of him. Yet.

"So where were you?" Jane asked.

"Let's go over to the others so I can tell you all at the same time. I can't stay long."

"You're not staying?! What's wrong?"

"Nettie," Hannah said, sounding both distressed and relieved. "Thank heavens you're back."

"Where did you go, dear?" her mother asked. "You didn't stay out all night, did you? What happened?"

"I went looking for William. And I ran into him eventually."

"Was he all right? What about his family?"

"They're fine. The fire didn't cause much damage, fortunately."

"Thank goodness," her mother sighed. "So did you stay with them?"

"I stayed with William," she said hesitantly. "But not at his parents'."

"Nettie, you didn't! I know you were mad at your father, and I don't even blame you for that. But to spend the night with a young man?"

"Mother, it was nothing like that." She paused, and then decided to just tell them the truth. "In fact... William and I got married last night."

Her mother's mouth dropped open, and Hannah was stunned. Only Jane was able to speak. She clapped her hands and laughed, "There I was joking about the fact you two hadn't even kissed properly, but then you run off and marry him!"

"Marry?" their father's voice bellowed from behind them. "What's this talk about marriage? Who got married?"

Nettie spun round in fright. His dark eyes sent murderous glares at her. She opened and closed her mouth, wondering what to say to him. But suddenly her mother stepped forward and manoeuvred herself in between her husband and her daughter.

"Henry dear, Nettie got married to William yesterday."

"She married that ragman's spawn? When?"

"I told you, yesterday."

"But when exactly?"

"Why, after you scared her out of our home obviously."

"I didn't scare anyone out of my home. The silly cow ran away."

"Only after you told her you'd set fire to the poor boy's house, you big oaf!"

"That doesn't mean she had to run off and marry the blighter, does it? You must be joking! Tell me you're only saying that to wind me up?"

Nettie stepped from behind her mother's back. "No, Father. It's true. William and I are married."

He stared at her, his face seemingly blank. For a moment, it looked like he wouldn't become angry. But then his eyes narrowed and one side of his mouth curled up in a vicious snarl.

"You absolute trollop! How could you? How dare you?"

His face turned red with anger, while bulbous veins popped out at his neck.

"Henry, calm down," his wife said. "Shouting won't help."

"I'll shout all I want, woman! When did this happen? Where? And who married you?"

"It happened last night," Nettie replied. She felt remarkably calm. As if his anger couldn't touch her. "We went to see Father Michael, we explained our situation and he immediately agreed to marry us in his church."

"I knew that blasted blackfrock would be involved. And I bet old man Kirby is behind it too. He put his son up to this. He must have."

"Father, no one put us up to anything. William and I love each other. We want to build a family and spend the rest of our lives together."

"Love," he scoffed. "You've been wasting too much time at those music halls of yours, listening to too many foolish songs. And what do you know about building a family?"

"I reckon I know more about love than you do," she snapped. "Your heart is as black as a hard lump of coal!"

"Insult me as much as you like, Nettie. Your words won't stop me."

He grabbed hold of her arm. "First, we'll go see the Kirbys. It's obvious my message yesterday wasn't clear enough."

"Let go of me," she hissed.

"And then we'll find that meddlesome priest and get him to annul this marriage. I never consented to it and it's probably not legal anyway."

"You can't!" She struggled against his tight grip. "It's too late. William and I are married, and there's nothing you can do about it."

"Just you wait and see," he grumbled as he pulled her along.

Chapter Thirty-Two

William's palms were sweaty when he stepped through the front door and into the dark and narrow corridor. He told himself all he needed to do was say goodbye and get his money. His mother would be upset of course, and his brothers were likely to be confused and worried when they heard he had somehow managed to get himself married the night before. But if he kept things short and he was quick about it, then his father wouldn't have a chance to cause much of a fuss.

Or so he hoped.

He took a deep breath and entered the kitchen. Both his brothers as well as his mother were sitting at the table, finishing their breakfast. His father was nowhere in sight.

"William!" The look of surprise on Joseph's face was immediately followed by a big smile.

He'd miss his little brother's smiles, William thought.

"Where's Father?"

"In the privies out back," Thomas replied, pointing with his thumb at the backyard. "We were just about to head out for the day. He was drunk last night, you see, so he slept late."

"Where were you?" Joseph asked with obvious concern.

"I was with Nettie," William smiled to reassure him.

His mother got up from her chair. "I thought you might be. She's a lovely girl. Have you had anything to eat yet?"

"No, I haven't. But that's not why I'm here. I have something to tell you all. Something important."

"Well, sit down and have some breakfast first, love. You must be starving. You can tell us while you're eating."

She set down some bread and butter for him on the table.

"I really haven't got much time," he said.

"Shall I fry you a few eggs as well?" she asked, ignoring his remark.

"And what's this news you wanted to tell us?" Joseph insisted.

William felt torn. He would have loved to sit down and break the news gently to them. And in a different world, he imagined they would then talk cheerfully for the rest of the morning, reminiscing about their years together and discussing his plans for the future.

But the longer he waited, the sooner his father would come walking back in. And he really wanted to retrieve his money before that happened. Maybe if he dashed into the bedroom now and did that first?

"Well, well. Look who's finally returned."

William squirmed. *Too late.*

"Been out drinking all night, have you? Hell of a moment you picked for it, what with that fire and all. You should have been at home, son. To protect the family in case that lowlife arsonist came back."

"I wasn't drinking."

"You weren't? Oh yeah, I forgot. You're not that kind of man, are you? Tell me, Will. What sort of a man are you then?"

William chose not to react. It was clear his father was still under the influence of the heavy drinking he had been doing the night before.

And that always tended to make him more unpredictable. More dangerous too.

"I didn't come here to argue with you," he said.

"Is that so? How awfully noble. Have you come to fill your belly at my table instead? You clear off without saying a word, when someone has tried to roast us like pigs on a spit. And then you come prancing back, expecting to be fed."

His father sat down. He pulled the bread and butter Mother had laid out for William towards himself and took a bite.

"But let me tell you something. I demand a full day's work out of you before you've earned any food from my table, do you hear? I won't tolerate idle good-for-nothings sponging off of my hard work."

William gritted his teeth. *Let it pass*, he told himself. He'd come here to say goodbye and get his money. And that's exactly what he would do. No arguing, no needless fighting.

His father continued eating William's bread. Mother had finished frying the eggs and she wanted to bring them over to William's place at the table. But his father snapped his fingers and gestured to give them to him instead. She obeyed silently, albeit while throwing him a dirty look.

"So where were you last night if you weren't out drinking?"

"If you must know, I was with Nettie."

"That market girl again? Hasn't she caused enough trouble already? You do realise it was probably her father who started the fire, don't you?"

"You have no proof of that." He didn't think it would be wise to tell his father what Nettie had shared the previous evening.

"I don't need proof. It's just the sort of dirty trick a filthy dog like him would pull. And then you run off for a night of fun with his daughter."

William sighed. "I haven't got time for this nonsense." He turned to go to the bedroom. But his father jumped up from his chair.

"Where do you think you're going?"

"I'm fetching my things. That's what I came here for. I'm leaving."

"Leaving?" his father said angrily.

His brothers gasped and his mother clenched her tea towel to her chest.

"How come you're leaving so suddenly?" his father demanded. "Has this market girl got anything to do with it?"

"Father—"

"Has she been whispering sweet words in your ear? Did she shake her hips and pout those pretty lips of hers at you?"

"You're a mean old man, do you know that?" William took two steps towards the door, but his father rushed over to him and grabbed his arm.

"What did you call me?"

William looked at his father's hand on his arm and then stared him dead in the eye. "I said you were mean."

"What's the matter?" his father snarled. "Did I hurt your precious feelings because I said something bad about your sweetheart?"

He knew his father was spoiling for a fight. It was the only language the man understood. But William refused to be drawn in.

"Let go," he said as he shook his arm free. "I'm getting my things and then I'll be out of your life forever."

His father still stood in William's way, keeping him from leaving the kitchen. "You're lost without me, you miserable weakling. You're not man enough to survive on your own. Or will you get your darling coster girl to look after you?"

"I can take care of myself. And in fact, I'll be looking after her. Nettie and I are going to be living together."

Don't tell him you're married, an inner voice urged. *He'd be furious with you and then you'll never get out of here without a fight. Go get your money!*

"I knew it," his father grinned viciously. "In that case, you're not taking your things with you. The clothes on your back will do."

"What?!"

"You don't own a thing in this house. Everything you have, you have because of me. And I'll be damned before I let you take any of it to run off with that harlot!"

"She's not a harlot!" He just about managed to stop himself from adding that Nettie was his wife. "Oh, fine. You can keep my things. They're nothing but worthless rags anyway. But I'm taking my money."

He tried to push past his father, but the old man kept blocking him.

"What money?"

"My money! The money I saved."

"Money you stole from me, more likely."

"I didn't steal any money from you. I earned that money myself."

"By hiding things from me and selling them yourself, no doubt. That money's rightfully mine and I'm not letting you have it."

"Let me through!"

"No," his father snarled, trying to grab his son's shirt.

When William swatted his father's hand away, the man immediately hit out with his other fist. But William managed to block the punch and instinctively hit back, ramming his own fist into his father's belly. Desperate to get to his money in the bedroom, he then gave his father an angry shove. Henry Kirby flew back and landed square on the kitchen table, which buckled under the force of the impact.

William's mother shrieked, while his brothers jumped to their feet.

"I'll teach you to raise your hand against me," his father grumbled, before throwing himself at William.

The two of them were grappling for each other's throat, when a piece of brick flew through the window. With a loud crash, it shattered the glass and landed on the kitchen floor.

"Kirby!" an angry voice shouted from outside. "Show yourself, you dustbin-crawling maggot! And bring your cowardly son out as well."

"The coster," William's father growled with a vicious scowl. He peered through the broken window into the courtyard at the back and grinned. "And he's brought his daughter along."

Chapter Thirty-Three

"Why did you have to throw a brick through their window?" Nettie hissed at her father. "Haven't you done enough damage to their home already?" You could still see the thick layer of black soot on the wall from the fire he had started the day before.

"Shut your mouth, Nettie. It's the only way to get these people's attention." He turned back to the house. "Kirby! Show yourself, I said!"

The back door opened and Mr Kirby stepped outside, but he kept his distance. William and his younger brothers soon followed. The expression on William's face told Nettie he felt just as miserable to be in this mess as she did.

"Here I am," Mr Kirby barked. "What do you want, Cabbage Face?"

"Kirby, I knew you were a nasty piece of work. And now it seems your son is just as bad."

"How do you know where I live?"

"Eh, what?" The question took Nettie's father off guard.

"How do you know where I live? I don't exactly remember ever telling you."

"I asked around," Nettie's father said, fidgeting with his hands. "You're quite well known in the area."

"That's because I'm a well-respected tradesman," Mr Kirby smirked.

"Someone with a reputation more like," Nettie's father scoffed.

"So you've never been here before, have you?"

"Uh..." Nettie's father looked around, visibly lost for words. "What?"

"You must be deaf, Cabbage Face. I asked if you've ever been here before." Mr Kirby looked at the soot on the wall and casually passed a finger along the blackened surface.

"Why would I?" Nettie's father said. "Nothing but robbers and ragmen down here. Why do you even ask?"

Nettie could hardly believe her father's cheek. And she suspected Mr Kirby would see right through this rather poor bluff.

Mr Kirby took a few steps towards Nettie and her father. "Oh, I only asked because some lunatic tried to set fire to my house yesterday.

And I was wondering if maybe you had anything to do with it."

He glared defiantly, his twinkling eyes daring her father to admit he did it.

"All those rags you've got piled up at the back of your filthy dwellings are a fire hazard, Kirby. I'm sure they catch fire real easily. It's a small miracle the whole building hasn't burned down several times yet."

Mr Kirby moved even closer, so that now their faces were merely a foot apart.

"You haven't answered my question. You're being suspiciously evasive, Cabbage Face."

"And you're distracting me from what I came here for this morning."

"Did you set fire to my house?"

"That's not why I'm here." He pointed at William. "I'm here for your son."

"What about him?" Mr Kirby didn't take his eyes off Nettie's father for a single second. "Answer my question: were you the scoundrel who set fire to my house?"

"Don't play innocent with me, Kirby. You know perfectly well what your son has done. It was probably you who set him up to it in the first place."

Mr Kirby briefly glanced over his shoulder at William. "What's he done then?"

"Stop pretending you don't know!"

"What are you talking about, man?"

Nettie's father looked at the sky and let out a loud, exasperated grunt. "Your peacock son married my daughter last night!"

To Nettie's surprise, Mr Kirby roared with laughter. She didn't know what kind of reaction she was expecting, but certainly not laughter.

"I thought vegetables were supposed to be good for you," Mr Kirby said. "But it's clear they've caused *you* to go out of your mind, coster. My son marrying your scraggy daughter? That's the most ridiculous thing I've ever heard."

"Oh, you feeble-brained imp! Ask him yourself then if you don't believe me."

Mr Kirby turned his head slightly towards his son. "William, Cabbage Face here says you married his ugly daughter."

William stepped forward and cleared his throat. "It's true, Father."

Mr Kirby spun round. "What?! When?"

"Late last night. Just like Mr Morris said."

"So it's 'Mr Morris' now, is it? Whose side are you on, you wretched traitor? This coster sets fire to our home and what do you do? You run to his scrawny daughter and you marry the wench. The very same night!"

"My daughter is not a wench, Kirby!"

"Yes, she is. I don't know what my lad sees in her, because she's clearly got her father's looks. But I'm sure she batted those eyelashes and wiggled that backside of hers. And Lord knows what else she did to him to make him lose his wits."

"You've got it all wrong, Kirby. It's your wicked son who seduced my poor daughter. Not the other way around. Your entire family is a bunch of degenerates."

"You take that back, Cabbage Face!"

"Make me, you... you bin sniffer."

Suddenly, Mr Kirby spat Nettie's father in the face. The oozing blob of mucus hit him right in the eye socket.

"You disgusting pig," Nettie's father squirmed as he desperately tried to wipe the spit off his face. "I should have done a better job and burned your house down to the ground with you and your son in it. Then none of this would have happened!"

"So it was you?!" Mr Kirby yelled. His hands flew towards Nettie's father's throat. "You'll pay for this, coster!"

The two men struggled as Mr Kirby tried to strangle Nettie's father while the latter punched at the hands on his throat and at Mr Kirby's head.

"Stop it," Nettie shrieked.

William grabbed his father from behind and pulled hard. Taken by surprise, Mr Kirby stumbled backwards and fell over.

"So that's how it is now, is it?" He glared at them while he sat on the ground. "The three of you against just me, eh?" Slowly, he rose to his feet again. "I guess I'll need a little help then."

He reached into his coat and when he pulled his hand back out, Nettie saw a flash of metal.

"He's got a knife," she gasped.

"Father, there's no need for that," William said, his body tense and on alert.

"Don't be a fool, Kirby," Nettie's father added, trying to keep his own gruffness in check.

"Not so brave now, are you?" Mr Kirby snarled, waving the knife in front of them. "Coming to my home, threatening me, assaulting me. I'll cut all three of you, do you hear? Slit your bloody throats, I will."

Still holding the knife in one hand, his eyes jumped between Nettie, her father and William, as if he was weighing his options. Was he only bluffing, she wondered fearfully?

"And I'll start with this one," he cried as he suddenly leapt at Nettie, thrusting his knife forwards.

"Father, no," William shouted while Nettie yelled in fright. He threw himself at Mr Kirby, grabbing hold of his father's arm.

"Traitor," Mr Kirby growled, furiously grappling with William to free his arm from his son's grip. "You're next. I swear I'll kill you next."

With all the scuffling and confusion, Nettie couldn't see the knife anymore. But she thought perhaps William was trying to wrestle it out of his father's hand.

Red with frenzied rage, Mr Kirby head-butted his son, making William's head spin for a short moment. Seizing his chance, the man lashed out with his fists.

Nettie heard William letting out a sharp roar of pain, and then it seemed as if the world stopped. Both William and his father stood frozen, while they stared at each other in disbelief.

William took two short, awkward steps back, while he clutched his belly with both his hands. His lips moved, but there was no sound.

Nettie looked down and she thought she would be sick when she saw the pool of red that was rapidly spreading around his hands.

Chapter Thirty-Four

"William," Nettie yelled in a high-pitched voice, dashing over. Standing before him, she wanted to do something, anything, to help him. But she didn't know what.

"Nettie," he groaned.

"Tell me what to do, my love," she whimpered as she gingerly touched his face and tears began to flow from her eyes.

"My legs."

His eyes rolled away into his head and he dropped to his knees. Nettie hurried to catch him and lowered him to the floor so he lay on his back. She sat down with him, holding his head in her lap. Dark red blood flowed from his belly and onto the ground around them.

She looked up and spotted his brothers, who were staring back at them in shock. "Joseph, Thomas. Go fetch a doctor, quick."

"Where? I don't know any doctors."

"Then find Father Michael instead. He'll know what to do. But hurry, please!"

Both boys ran off as fast as they could. "You go to the church, I'll try the market," Thomas called.

"Nettie?" William's voice sounded weak.

"I'm here, my love."

"Where? I can't... I can hardly see you." His eyes had trouble focussing as they searched for her. He lifted up a feeble hand. She took it, kissed it and pressed it against her face so he would feel her.

"I'm right here by your side, my darling," she said with a trembling and tearful voice. "Father Michael is on his way. Are you in pain?"

"No," he frowned, looking up at the sky. "I don't feel much pain. I don't feel much of anything."

Nettie didn't think that was a good sign. "You stay with me now, William. The doctor will take care of you."

"Nettie?"

"Yes, my love?"

"I'm dying."

"No, you're not. You mustn't. You can't die. We're only just married. You have all these plans for the future, remember? Our future."

"It's getting so dark, Nettie. What time is it?"

"I don't know, my love. But Father Michael will be here any minute, you'll see."

"Strange. I can hear your voice, but it's as if I'm seeing you through a thick fog. There's this grey haze covering everything."

"That's fine, my love. If you can still hear me, then just listen to my voice, all right? You listen to my voice and stay with me."

"I feel tired, Nettie. Like I'm falling asleep."

"No, don't fall asleep! Keep your eyes open."

"I can't. My eyelids... so heavy."

His eyes closed and Nettie panicked.

"William? William, look at me. William, please. I love you."

He tried to smile as his eyes flickered open again. "I love you too, my darling Nettie."

"Good," she said. "That's good." She had to keep him talking, she knew. But the words were escaping her. What do you say to someone who's bleeding to death in your arms? "We still need to find a room, you know."

"A room?"

"We were going to look for a room today, remember? A small room for you and me. Just for now." She found herself gently rocking her upper body back and forth. "Until we both find work and have the money to rent something nicer. That's what you said. That's our plan."

"Our plan, yes."

"Exactly."

"Nettie?"

"Yes, dearest?"

"When I'm gone–"

"Don't say that. Please don't."

"You have to ask Thomas about my money. He'll give it to you."

"I don't want your money, William. You know that. I want you! You're my husband now."

"I'm sorry to make a widow out of you so soon."

"No, you won't. I can't be a widow when you're still alive."

"I love you, Nettie."

His eyes were closing again.

"And I love you too, William. Please don't die."

"Goodbye, my love. I'll always–"

His voice trailed off and his head slowly rolled to the side.

"No-o-o," Nettie wailed. "William!"

There was a clatter of metal on cobblestone, as Mr Kirby dropped his knife. Mortified with shock and grief, he stumbled backwards, staring wide-eyed at the dying figure of his son. When his back hit the wall, he slid down and sat on the ground.

"What have I done?" he muttered incredulously. "Sweet baby Jesus, what have I done?"

"Ha," Nettie's father scoffed scornfully. "Killed your own son, that's what you've done! You stupid imbecile. You wanted to stab my daughter, but instead you've murdered your son. Wait until I tell this one to all the lads at The Boar's Head!"

His laughter bounced off the walls of the houses surrounding the small courtyard. The sound felt like torture to Nettie's ears.

"Shut up, Father," she blurted out angrily. "Please, just shut up and stop talking. This isn't a joke, you know!"

He seemed taken aback by the sudden forcefulness of her outburst. But it had the desired effect of silencing him.

"You're as much to blame for this as Mr Kirby," she snapped.

"Me? But I didn't–"

"Yes, you! You and your big mouth. You and your fancy ideas. You and your stupid pride."

Nettie felt wounded to her very core. She had heard about broken hearts before, but this was infinitely more than that. It was as if a part of her had been ripped out. In her chest and in her belly, she felt a deep and viciously burning pain that seemed to want to consume her.

And this pain fuelled her anger towards her father.

"Can't you see?" she shouted at him as bitter tears streamed down her face. "Can't you see what you've done? You and William's father, you're one and the same. You hardly know each other and yet you despise each other with a passion stronger than the deadliest poison."

From somewhere within her, a raw scream of anguish came welling up. She let it out, allowing all the rage and the fury to leave her body with it. All she was left with in its wake was a maddening sense of complete emptiness.

"And now, William is dead," she said, her voice almost emotionless. "Because he's the son of a ragman and you have this delusion in your head that only costermongers are decent folk. I've lost my husband because of the silly games you and Mr Kirby have been playing all your lives."

Her father opened his mouth. But he didn't know what to say. For the first time ever, he realised words were meaningless.

Sitting motionless against the wall, the only sound coming from William's father was a muffled and pitiful weeping noise as he buried his crying face in his hands.

"Make way," Father Michael called to the small crowd of curious onlookers who had gathered. He came running into the courtyard with two men carrying a stretcher.

"Good Lord," he gasped when he saw Nettie and William, surrounded by a pool of blood. "What in heaven's name has happened here?"

"It was an accident," Mr Kirby sobbed. "I never meant to hurt him."

"Father," Nettie begged with tears in her eyes. "I think William's dead."

The priest knelt down next to her and touched two fingers to William's neck. "No," he said after a brief pause. "I can still feel a pulse. It's faint, but it's there. We need to get William to our hospital. Quickly." He gestured to his men. "Put him on the stretcher. Careful."

While the men cautiously transferred William onto the stretcher, Father Michael offered Nettie a hand to help her get up from the ground.

"Come with me, child. Your poor William may yet survive. But it will be up to the skill of the surgeon and the grace of our good Lord."

Chapter Thirty-Five

With all the colour gone from his face, William looked frightfully pale as he lay in his bed at the small hospital run by Father Michael and the nuns. There were nine other beds on the ward, all of them occupied by people of varying ages. Screens had been placed on both sides of William's bed, to afford him a bit more peace and a sense of shelter.

His eyes were closed and Nettie didn't know if he was merely asleep or unconscious. He hadn't responded to her or anyone else since he slipped away from her in the courtyard behind his home.

Now, she sat on a chair by his side, holding his hand and staring at him with empty eyes while a struggle between hope and despair was going on in her mind. She thought a grimace of pain and discomfort covered William's otherwise gentle face. As if he was having a bad dream.

A bad dream we're all caught up in, she lamented silently.

"Mercifully, none of his vital organs were ruptured," the surgeon explained to both families, who were standing at the end of the bed with Father Michael. "But he's lost an awful lot of blood and we might still lose him."

Mary Kirby let out a little sob and quickly covered her mouth with a handkerchief.

"I know it sounds grim," the surgeon said. "But I wouldn't wish to give you any false hope. His wound has been disinfected, stitched and bandaged. All we can do now is pray."

"Then that is what we shall do," Father Michael spoke softly. "Together. Thank you, doctor, for your efforts. Come, let me escort you to the door."

The surgeon put on his hat and nodded at the families, who meekly mumbled their thanks. When he and Father Michael had left the ward, an uncomfortable silence fell over the small group. Nettie's parents stood at one corner of the bed, while William's parents were on the other corner. Physically, only a few feet separated them. But Nettie suspected it must have felt like a gaping abyss between them.

Serves them right, she thought. *Let them squirm for a bit. It might just do them some good.*

A casual glance over her shoulder showed her their families would need more than an awkward silence to turn things around however.

Both her father and Mr Kirby appeared too ashamed to look at each other or even at William. Instead, their eyes searched the ceiling and the walls of the ward, as if things far more interesting had caught their attention there.

Mary Kirby still stood sobbing softly into her handkerchief, but Nettie's mother was glaring darkly at her own husband.

Nettie sighed and turned back to William. *Hopeless*, she told herself. William had been right. Their parents would never change. She and him had had their chance of freedom. They could have escaped this bleak life and started something new, something better and more beautiful.

But that was over now.

She started crying and lowered her head onto William's shoulder. *Please don't make me do this alone, my love. I don't want to.*

"Well?" Nettie's mother asked, clearly annoyed.

"Well what?" Nettie's father replied sheepishly.

"When are you finally going to apologise, Henry?"

"Apologise? For what? And to whom?"

"To Mr and Mrs Kirby! For the dirty part you've played in this sad and tragic mess."

"But Harriet, I–"

"And to your own daughter! For having caused her so much grief. All the girl did was fall in love."

"You don't understand. I only–"

"You only what, Henry? Did what you had to do, I suppose?"

"I merely wanted to keep her from getting hurt. To protect her from harm."

"Then you have the oddest way of protecting people, Henry Morris! Setting fire to a poor family's home? Some hero you are!"

Over at the other corner of the bed, Mr Kirby chuckled at the dressing-down his adversary was receiving.

"What's so funny, George?" his wife suddenly snapped.

"Nothing, dear."

"Then why did I just hear that noise coming out of your stupid throat?" She hit him over the head with her handkerchief. "It sounded like you were laughing to me. Do you feel there's anything to laugh at here?"

"No, of course not, dear," he whimpered.

"No, there isn't, is there? All I see is our son lying half-dead in a hospital bed. And who put him there, George? You did! You plunged a knife in my boy's belly, you monster!"

"That was an accident! I never intended to hurt him."

"No, you wanted to kill the boy's newlywed wife instead."

"He wanted to slit all three of our throats in fact," Nettie's father piped up. "He said so."

Harriet Morris slapped the back of her husband's head and followed that up with a punch to the nose. "You stay out of this, Henry! I don't want to hear another word from you."

"I was only telling–"

Nettie's mother boxed his ears. "Be quiet, I said. Your words have brought me and our family more than enough misery over the years. I've had it with your waffling and your laziness."

She placed her hands on her hips, as her eyes shot glaring thunderbolts at him. "And I'll tell you another thing. From now on, if you have another one of your bright ideas, you ask me for permission first. Do you hear?"

"Yes, dear."

"That goes for you as well, George," Mary Kirby joined in. "The boys and I have suffered at your hands for long enough. Each single one of our lads is far smarter than you and I combined. And it's time you let them go their own way."

"But–"

"And if that means they want to marry someone whose father you have an issue with, then that's your problem, not theirs."

"Well spoken, Mrs Kirby," Nettie's mother said.

"It's clear our husbands can't think straight, Mrs Morris. So I guess we'll have to do the thinking for them."

"Exactly. Having said that, Henry, I still haven't heard an apology from you."

"You too, George."

There was a brief silence while both men swallowed their pride. Mr Kirby was the first to speak.

"I'm sorry I threatened you with a knife, Morris. And I'm sorry for attacking your daughter. I wasn't being myself."

"You were angry because I tried to set fire to your house. That's understandable. I never should have done that. I'm sorry."

"Guess I shouldn't have stolen your pots and pans to begin with." He cleared his throat. "I also want to apologise for all the ugly things I called your daughter. I didn't mean it. I'm sure she's a lovely girl."

"And I should have given your son a fair chance. If my Nettie fell in love with him, that must mean he's a fine chap."

"Good," Nettie's mother said. "Now shake hands and look each other in the eye while you do. You'll see it'll be like looking in a mirror. The two of you are more alike than you think."

"That's right," Mary Kirby said. "Bloody fools, both of you."

The two men reached out and shook hands, a bit awkwardly at first but then more firmly, as they began to realise just how right their wives had been.

"Nettie," William croaked.

She looked up at him and instantly sat up straight. His eyes were open!

"William!" She brought his hand to her lips and pressed a kiss on it. "William, thank God. Talk to me. Say something, please."

"Nettie, am I dead?"

"No, of course not. You're alive, my love."

"I thought I'd died and gone to heaven... when I saw my father and yours standing there, shaking hands."

His parents rushed over to the other side of the bed, while Nettie's parents came and stood behind her.

"I was afraid I'd lost you, son," Mr Kirby said. "All because of my temper."

William tried to smile at his father. There was no reproach on his face, only forgiveness.

"And I came close to losing my daughter. Like an idiot, I nearly drove her away." He placed a hand on her shoulder. "Nettie dearest, can you forgive your foolish father?"

She lay her hand over his and nodded her head, overcome with tears.

"And while we're on the topic of forgiveness," Mr Kirby said. For the first time, he looked into her eyes. The angry and vicious Mr Kirby she had seen so many times seemed like a different man than the person who stood before her now. "Nettie, I've treated you very unfairly. But if you can find it in your heart to forgive me, I swear I will try to be a good father-in-law to you. Welcome to our family, dear."

Smiling faintly, William lifted up his hand above his sheets and they all joined hands over his.

"Now there's a sight to behold," Father Michael spoke breathlessly. He had returned and stood watching them with twinkling eyes and a mesmerised look on his face. "This is more beautiful and more moving than the prettiest nativity scene I've ever laid eyes on."

"Oh, Father Michael," Nettie said, warm tears of joy rolling down her cheeks. "Isn't it wonderful?"

She looked back at William. Through the gateway of their eyes, the two of them stared deep into each other's soul. And in that moment, they knew in their hearts that they had a bright future together.

A future filled with love, laughter and all manner of abundance.

Epilogue

The doorbell tinkled its bright tune when Nettie entered the antiques shop near closing time. William was busy showing a vase to a customer, telling the fashionably dressed lady all about the object's history and pointing out little details of the remarkable craftsmanship that had gone into it. Nettie smiled. She knew this was the part of shopkeeping that he enjoyed the most. And she loved watching his fine salesmanship at work.

"Good afternoon, Mrs Kirby," the young shop assistant greeted her kindly. "Lovely to see you."

"Hello, Archie. And how are you today?"

"Very well, Mrs Kirby. I sold a silver tea set this morning!"

"Did you now? Well done, Archie."

"Thank you, Mrs Kirby. When the customer enquired about a tea set, I asked Mr Kirby to come over. But Mr Kirby said he felt sure I was quite capable of serving the gentleman myself."

"And so you were, evidently." Nettie smiled fondly at how proud he seemed of his achievement. She remembered how timid and insecure the boy from the slums had been when he first joined them as an apprentice. Personally selected by Father Michael, the priest had assured them Archie would make a great addition to their staff. And he'd been right.

"Mr Kirby tells me you'll be visiting the old neighbourhood this evening?"

"Yes, Father Michael has invited us to come and see the new hospital ward he's opened up."

"Thanks to generous donations from you and Mr Kirby, I'm told."

"We try to help, I suppose."

"You're much too modest, Mrs Kirby. My mother says you two are a pair of angels."

Nettie laughed. "Oh, I don't know about that."

"No, it's true. You do so much for us. Plenty of other people in your fortunate position would simply enjoy their success and forget all about the East End."

"Life has been very good to us. So Mr Kirby and I feel it's our duty to give something back."

"Archie," William called over. "Will you carefully wrap the vase this lady has just purchased, please?"

"Certainly, sir." He nodded politely at Nettie. "Excuse me, Mrs Kirby."

After the customer had paid William, he came over to his wife, wearing that special smile of his.

"Hello, my beloved," he said with a twinkle in his eye. "How are you and James both doing today?"

Nettie's hand stroked her pregnant belly. "We don't know if it's going to be another boy, dear. I wouldn't mind having a girl this time."

"John and David can be quite the handful, can't they?" he chuckled. "I bet you're happy to be out of the house for a while. Poor nanny though, having to look after two bouncy toddlers like them."

"Your mother is with them as well. She visited for tea this afternoon and kindly offered to stay until we're back from our visit to Father Michael."

"I'm pleased she and the children like each other so much. Ever since my father died, she's been a bit lost."

They looked up when the doorbell sounded as the customer left the shop with her vase.

"Time to close up, I should think," William said. "Archie, will you be coming with us? We're taking the horse tram."

"Oh no, sir. I'll walk."

"All the way home?"

The boy seemed embarrassed. "Walking's cheaper, Mr Kirby. I give most of my wages to my mother and I try to save up as much of the rest as I can."

"But you'll need new soles for your shoes in no time that way," William laughed. "Ride the tram with us, Archie. We'll pay your fare."

"Are you sure, Mr Kirby?" the boy asked, his eyes wide in astonishment.

"Of course we're sure, Archie," Nettie said.

"Thank you, Mr Kirby. And Mrs Kirby." He blushed and asked, "May I sit at the top then? I've never been on a horse tram before, but the view up there must be great!"

"You may sit wherever you like, my dear boy. But I hope you understand Mrs Kirby and I won't be climbing those stairs with you in Mrs Kirby's condition."

"Of course, sir!" He blushed at the hint of Nettie's pregnancy and she tried not to smile. His innocence was so sweet.

Just over an hour later, the three of them alighted from the tram at the stop closest to Father Michael's.

"Do you think you'll manage the last bit, my darling?" William asked, full of loving concern. "Perhaps I should hail a carriage."

"Don't be silly, William. It's probably not more than fifteen minutes. I'm perfectly capable of walking that far, you know. I'm merely with child, not crippled," she teased. "Besides, the weather is fine and I think I should like to take a short stroll."

"I'll run ahead," Archie said. "And tell Father Michael you're on your way." Their apprentice dashed off, leaving them to walk at their own leisurely pace and enjoy each other's company.

"These streets have changed, don't you think?" William asked as he looked around.

"They have. But some things are still the same. The people still look as poor, dirty and malnourished as when you and I lived here." Watching a little girl in rags crossing the filthy street on her bare feet, Nettie sighed. "There's so much work left to do."

"We do what we can, my love. We sold two vases and a brass candelabra today. And did Archie tell you about the silver tea set he sold?"

"He did. He seemed so proud."

"Yes, we made a tidy profit today." He patted the wallet tucked away in the pocket of his vest. "And I've brought some of it along to give to Father Michael."

"He'll be so happy."

Seemingly out of nowhere, a gaggle of boys appeared around them, some of them holding out their hand. "Have you got a coin or two to spare, guv? We're so hungry. Our brothers and sisters too."

"Of course," William said while he reached into his pockets for some coins. But Nettie felt a cold tingle at the back of her neck. There was something about this group she didn't like. Their leader looked about fourteen years old, and already he had a hard, calculated stare in his eyes. She tensed up and felt herself grasping her husband's arm a bit more tightly.

"There you go, lads," William said when he had given them a few shiny small coins.

"Thanks, guv," the leader replied. "Now how about handing over the rest as well?" In his hand he held a piece of wood with a rusty nail through it. "You wouldn't want us to hurt your precious lady, would you?"

"Yeah," another boy grinned menacingly. "It'd be a shame if we had to prick her." He was holding a nasty looking shard of glass dangerously close to Nettie's belly.

Her nerves were screaming in her throat and she broke out in a cold sweat. *Not my unborn baby*, she prayed silently. They could take all their money, all their wealth and even their beautiful home away from her. But not her children. *Please, Lord!*

"Oi oi!" a voice shouted.

Something hard hit the temple of the leader's head, making him yell out in pain. Everyone turned and saw a handful of boys across the street. One of them had a sling and after he had shot another stone at the street muggers, they all charged.

"I thought we told you never to come here again," the eldest of the rescuers growled.

Since the leader of the muggers was still whimpering with pain from his head wound, the gang of street rats quickly scattered away.

"Sorry, Mr Kirby," the eldest boy said. "Are you all right? Are you hurt? Did those miserable thugs get anything?"

William looked at Nettie who was taking deep breaths to lower her frantic heartbeat and calm down the terrified baby in her womb.

"We're fine, lad. Just had a bit of a fright, that's all."

"Mr Kirby!" Father Michael called out. Together with Archie, the priest came running down the street, his black frock flapping behind him.

"Sweet heavens, what happened? Are you all right?"

"Some boys from Old Lane tried to mug them, Father," the boy explained.

"Good Lord! I'm so terribly sorry."

"It's fine, Father. We are unharmed. Aren't we, Nettie?"

She nodded and smiled, as some colour slowly started to return to her face.

"I shouldn't have invited you to come down here," Father Michael said. "It's too dangerous. When they see you, some folks might think you're an easy target."

"Nonsense," William insisted.

"Father Michael is right, Mr Kirby. It's not safe. Why don't you tell Archie to let me and the lads know in advance next time you come?"

"So *you* can mug us instead, you mean?" William laughed. Nettie knew her husband was kidding, but the boy looked genuinely shocked at the suggestion.

"Oh no, sir! We'd never do that, Mr Kirby. Besides," –smiling awkwardly, he scratched his head underneath his cap– "if we let that sort of thing happen, the ghost of your late father might come to haunt us."

"I think you might be right there, my lad!"

Everybody laughed, clearing the last remnants of the dreadful tension they had been feeling.

"Well, now that you have your own escort," Father Michael quipped, "shall we be on our way? I'm dying to show you those new beds we've been able to purchase thanks to your support."

William offered Nettie his arm again and she gladly slipped her hand around it. Walking with Father Michael while being surrounded by a group of noisily chatting boys, she stole a lovestruck glance at her husband. With him by her side, it didn't matter what life would throw at them.

But her heart also told her: life was through with throwing bad things their way. They were blessed. And for that, she felt eternally grateful.

The End

Continue reading...

If you enjoyed this book, you will love Hope Dawson's other romance stories as well.

Visit www.hopedawson.com for updates and to *claim your free digital book*.

Other titles by Hope:

The Forgotten Daughter
The Carter's Orphan
The Millworker's Girl
The Ratcatcher's Daughter
The Foundling With The Flowers
The Pit Brow Sisters
The Dockside Orphans
The Christmas Foundling
The Girl Below Stairs

Printed in Great Britain
by Amazon